DIVIDING
LINES

A novel by
Neil Blower

FIRESTEP
Press

IN LOVING MEMORY OF SGT
STEVEN 'TC' ROBERTS –
THE MAN WHO TAUGHT ME
NOT JUST TO BE A GOOD
SOLDIER, BUT A GOOD MAN AS
WELL.
THANK YOU, SARGE.

About the author

Neil Blower is the author of critically-acclaimed novel Shell Shock: The diary of Tommy Atkins. A former frontline soldier who saw bloody action in Kosovo and Iraq, he turned to writing "as a form of creative therapy" upon leaving the army in 2005 — after being diagnosed with post-traumatic stress disorder (PTSD).

He has been described as a "modern day Ernest Hemingway" and is affectionately known as the 'Lowry of Literature' in his home town of Salford, Greater Manchester, where he lives with his partner and two sons.

Follow Neil Blower on Twitter @neilbauthor and visit his website www.neilblower.com

FireStep Publishing
Gemini House
136-140 Old Shoreham Road
Brighton
BN3 7BD

www.firesteppublishing.com

First published by FireStep Press, an imprint
of FireStep Publishing in 2013

ISBN 978-1-908487-47-6

A CIP catalogue reference for this book is
available in the British Library.

Cover by Ryan Gearing
Typeset by Graham Hales, Derby

Contents

Acknowledgements

My thanks once again to Ryan Gearing and everyone at FireStep for supporting my work and me. To Vicky for her expert editorial guidance and cleaning up parts of the text. Special thanks go to Mr. E, (he knows who he is) for all his help and advice in regards to my research and making sure everything was correct. I could not have written the book without him!

Special thanks also go to Jon Kirk, Anthony Harvison and the team at Palamedes PR, for all their advice, support and the nurturing of my career. I could not wish for a better publicist.

And last but not least, my family: Sammie, Ethan and Oliver, without them there's not really much point in anything.

Thank you.

For Sammi, Ethan and Oliver
– the people who give my life
meaning.

You have your way. I have my way.
As for the right way, the correct way,
and the only way, it does not exist.

Friedrich Nietzsche (1844 – 1900)

1

10,000 Years Ago

In the beginning there was light. The laws of the universe, however, dictate that everything must have an opposite. Hot and cold. Up and down. Wet and dry. North and south. Positive and negative. Night and day. Good and evil. Everything has an opposite, and the opposite of light – is darkness.

The darkness was everywhere, it covered every corner of the jungle, and right now it inhabited every corner of his soul.

He was running, running, running. He had purpose, he felt alive.

This must be how the animals felt when they went in for the kill. He was a predator, and tonight he would find his prey.

He came to a clearing and stopped. He squinted while his eyes adjusted to the new source of light coming from the village a few hundred yards below him. His vision cleared and he saw movement… he saw them, dancing in the firelight. The enemy.

He hated them. They were different, they worshipped different gods – they stole his village's crops. They had to be destroyed. It was war.

The shamans of his village said that they had angered the gods. That was why the season's crops had yielded very little food. It was their fault that his young were starving. The shamans said that the gods wanted them to destroy the other village and take their food. It was the only way to protect their home and way of life.

The shamans were the wisest men in the village; they had power and wisdom and everyone followed their teachings. They were never wrong – how could they be – they talked to the gods?

As he knelt under the cover of darkness and the jungle, he looked to his left, then right. All the other men from his village were lying in wait. It was nearly time.

He had a feeling in his stomach, but it wasn't hunger – it was something else. Did the other warriors feel like this – or was it just him?

The enemy's village was almost identical to their own. He noticed that the way they had positioned their huts was very similar to theirs. Why had they done this?

As he waited for the signal to attack, his thoughts drifted to his own village, to his wife and children. His son and daughter would be asleep now; his wife would be waiting anxiously with the other women of the village for their return. He thought of his crops and his animals.

Then the signal came, and they attacked. As one, the men of his village surged forward and let out their battle cry.

He was running again, and he felt the soft earth beneath his feet and the wind in his face. He felt alive. The spear he held was brought up, ready for the kill. He kept his shield close to his chest for protection.

As he got nearer to the enemy's village he could make out shapes in the darkness, lit up by the fires. They seemed huge. The enemy was coming.

A shape sped towards him. He readied his spear and as the shape leapt on him, he plunged his spear into it. He felt it go all the way in. He felt the soft inside of the shape through the shaft of his spear and heard the sound it made. It was like carving meat.

The shape fell to the floor, taking the spear with it. For a moment he gazed on its face. It was like his.

He quickly pulled out the spear and continued on into the village. Chaos reigned. All around he could hear screams of pain, panic and fear.

He looked around for more enemies to fight. Another shape ran towards him. It leapt and again he raised his spear. This time the shape's blood spurted across his face. He plunged the spear in further until the shape stopped moving. He removed his weapon and searched for another target.

From nowhere something hit him and knocked him to the ground, face first. He rolled over and a shape flew at him, its spear pointed at his heart. He raised his shield and the shape landed. The point of the spear was almost touching his nose. The shape tried to force it further down, but he was too strong for it. He pushed the shape clear off him, picked up his own spear and went in for the kill, dispatching the shape quickly. As he removed the spear from its chest, he paused. Something about this one was different. He looked down on the body of his enemy. Then he realised... it was a woman.

Why had she attacked him? Women were not warriors; it was the men who fought battles. The shamans said that men hunted and protected the village and the women bore children and looked after the home. He wondered if this woman had any children. Where was her husband?

The battle was over. Behind him he could hear the victory cries of his fellow warriors and he looked around the enemy's village. It was decimated. Bodies lay everywhere – even the children had not been spared, or the women.

He wondered how any of this would help his crops grow. Would the gods be pleased at this and reward his village? The shamans came out from their position in the jungle from which they had watched the battle from a safe distance; the gods did not want them to fight – that was a warrior's job.

The chief of his village and the most powerful shaman walked among the ruins. The shaman whispered something in the chief's ear and the chief smiled, then declared that a great victory had taken place this day. The gods were pleased and they would all be rewarded.

The chief told all the warriors that they could search the enemy village and take what they wanted – tools, weapons, clothing, even food. The warrior wondered how any of this would help his crops grow.

* * *

Many centuries later the human race had evolved and adapted. More and more villages came into existence – which became towns – which became cities – which became nations.

Religions came and went. The belief in many gods made way for the belief in one true god. Other religions came along and prophets and saviours were born that left mankind with rules and words from god.

Empires rose. Laws were passed, broken and rewritten according to the rulers of the time. Empires fell. Others rose. Systems were invented to organise the human race – politics, philosophy, the arts. Financial systems evolved along with taxes, mortgages and business.

The human race made tools to aid them – first to hunt, then to farm. To build… and then to kill.

Mankind's thirst for bloodshed and violence was more often than not the key to progress. For every new discovery, people found a way of turning it into an instrument of death. And, ironically, the desire to destroy each other fuelled scientific exploration.

The world became smaller; wars became bigger. Mankind fought over everything – politics, religion, language, skin colour. They had many reasons for killing each other but most often, when the excuses were stripped away, all that was left was power, and greed.

Millennia passed and mankind didn't change. Conventional wisdom said that the human race had progressed from the times of old – we were civilised and had amassed a great amount of knowledge and wisdom. The people who said this were mostly the privileged with full bellies and a safe, secure living environment. But try saying that human beings are civilised to the millions who are starving, being raped, tortured and butchered in their homes for reasons beyond their understanding. The human race is a funny thing. On one side of the planet millions starve to death every day, while on the other, more civilised side of the globe, men of science are busy restricting people's stomachs so they can't eat themselves to death.

After thousands of years as the dominant species on the planet, mankind entered the 20th century, which brought the most rapid advance of progress ever known. The car, the plane, the radio, television, computers, the jet engine, the splitting of the atom. Humanity's knowledge expanded to the furthest reaches of the universe and to the tiniest sub-atomic particle – but it took the two biggest wars in history and half a century of being on the brink of annihilation to get there.

During the largest war in history, as the Allies advanced through Europe, a young soldier found himself alone. He sat against the wall as mortar and dust rained down on his helmet.

There was no way out – he was surrounded. Scared, alone, he was the only one left.

He checked his rifle. Empty. He pushed his head back against the wall, again, and again. He felt the hot tears begin to run down his face. It couldn't end like this; not like this. Still so much left to do. His thoughts drifted to home. Mum and dad, family, friends… her. Her smile. Her laugh. He'd never see her again. He'd never see anyone again. This was it – no way out.

He surveyed the bodies which lay around him. He saw Smithy and smiled – always late for parade, always in rag order – now torn apart by hot metal, travelling faster than sound. Not like this. Not like this. You're going to die. You are going to die. There's nothing you can do. They will be here any minute.

He looked around for some sign of hope. The boss's pistol, was it? The young soldier reached across to the carcass of his commander and grabbed the pistol from his hand. A full mag! His thoughts returned to home, then he stared at his friends around him. I don't want to die. Oh God, I don't want to die. He looked at the pistol, then at his friends. Unfastening his helmet, he dropped it on the floor and shrugged off his equipment, then got to his feet and walked outside. The hot sun forced him to squint as he raised the pistol and fired.

'The lord is my shepherd; I shall not want…'

Still walking, he fired again.

'He leadeth me in the paths of righteousness for his name's sake.'

Again he fired.

'YEA, THOUGH I WALK THROUGH THE VALLEY OF THE SHADOW OF DEATH!'

He fired again.

'I WILL FEAR NO EVIL!!'

And again.

'FOR THOUGH ART WITH ME!!!'

And again. He couldn't see for the tears. Could hardly breath.

'THY ROD AND THY STAFF, THEY COMFORT ME!!!!'

He fired again – empty.

Crying, he dropped to his knees. 'I don't want to die.' He didn't feel the bullets enter his body. He didn't feel a thing. He thought only of her.

* * *

Half a century later, in the middle of the last decade of the 20th Century, after sixty years of peace – on a world-wide scale – on a small island that used to run the world, a little boy played in the back garden of his grandparents' house, where his parents had brought him for a visit. The summer sun felt nice and warm on his bare legs. The rare fine weather had prompted his granddad to light the barbecue, and the grown ups were inside, preparing the food and having a drink.

The little boy played with his figures; Wolverine and Banshee were having a fight, which Wolverine was winning. On the TV show that morning, the bad guy was Magneto, but he didn't have him, though.

Suddenly there was thunder – the loudest he'd ever heard. But it wasn't cloudy. Why was there thunder? He heard his granddad shout from inside.

'What the bloody hell was that?'

His parents and grandparents came outside, and the next-door neighbours came out into their gardens.

'Did you hear that?'

'Yeah.'

'What was it?'

'Look, over there – is that smoke?'

'Jesus!'

The adults went round to the front garden and the boy followed. In the distance a plume of smoke was rising over the horizon.

'That's coming from town, that,' said one of them.

'What do you think – an explosion?'

'God knows. Put the telly on – see if it's on the news.'

'What do you think it was, Dad?' the little boy asked.

'I don't know, son. Could be a lot of things.'

The boy followed his father into the house, where his nana was struggling with the remote.

'How do you work this thing?'

'Give it 'ere,' said his granddad. He put the telly on and found the news... It should have been football. The boy watched the adults, who were all staring at the telly like zombies.

'Bomb... Manchester city centre... claimed responsibility... unknown injuries...'

'Oh God,' his mum said, as she started to cry.

'Bastards,' said his granddad, bitterly.

'Woss 'appened,' the little boy asked.

'A bomb has gone off in town, and a lot of people are hurt.'

'Is anyone dead?'

'They don't know yet.'

'He shouldn't be watching this,' said his nana.

'Go play in the garden, sweetheart. We'll be out in a minute,' said his mother.

'OK.'

The little boy made his way out through the kitchen and into the warmth of the garden. He could see the smoke that still hung over the houses, like a huge dirty snake in the sky.

He went into his granddad's shed, picked up his Man United football and started practicing his kick-ups. He couldn't get it to his head yet, though some of his friends could.

His mum came outside, watched him doing his kick-ups for a while, then came over and gave him a hug, squeezing him tight.

'I love you so much, little man.'

She kissed him on the cheek.

'I love you too, mum,' he answered.

'Strange,' he thought, and went back to his kick-ups, then his granddad came outside.

'Just spoke to Sheila. The boys are OK, but they had to wait for a phone box to call home and say they were all right. They'll have to walk back, though, because they've stopped all public transport – there are no buses or trains.'

'Oh, thank God. Just glad they're OK,' said his mum.

'Are you talking about Scott and Chris?' he asked. His older cousins went to town most Saturdays with their friends.

'Yes, sweetheart. They went to town with their mates – to the pictures, I think. Auntie Shelia has been on the phone to us, and they're OK.'

'Oh,' said the little boy.

'Right, time for some food.' His granddad went back into the house and came out with a plate of burgers, sausages and chicken and started to put them on the barbecue.

'Do you want another drink, darling?'

'Please mum.'

She went into the house and he went over to where his granddad was putting burgers on the barbecue.

'Granddad…'

'Yes.'

'Why does the IRA want to bomb us?'

His grandfather looked at him as he adjusted the burgers.

'Ask your dad.'

The little boy's dad came out of the house with two cans of beer and gave one to his granddad.

'He wants to know why the IRA want to bomb us. Thought I'd leave that to you'

'Thank you for that,' his dad replied. The little boy stood by the barbecue, waiting for his father to explain what had just happened. His father took a swig from his can of beer and looked at his son for a moment.

'It's a very complicated situation.'

'Why?'

'It just is. This has been going on for years. It's all to do with religion.'

'HA!' snorted his grandfather. His father fixed his own father with a strange look.

'It all goes back to when we ran Ireland.'

'What do you mean?' said the little boy.

'Well, you know how uncle Jim has his own business?'

'Yeah.'

'His firm fixes people's houses and puts extensions on them.'

'Right.'

'But he also owns the taxi firm, even though he's not a taxi-driver and he doesn't work at their office, he still gets the profits – the money that's left over after the drivers have been paid and all the other costs.'

'What's that got to with it?'

'Well, it was the same with Ireland a long time ago. Britain used to own the country and take the profits, but left the people who actually lived there very little. Not just money, but food as well.'

'I don't understand.'

'Not many people do! Even the politicians... useless idiots,' his granddad added.

'Anyway. So with Uncle Jim's taxi firm, what do you think would be fair?' his father asked.

The boy thought for a moment.

'Well, the drivers should run the firm, and then share the profits equally. That's the fairest way. They do all the work, so they should get the most.'

'That's exactly what the people of Ireland thought.'

'So what happened?'

'They got what they wanted. They became independent – a separate country.'

'So what about the IRA? Why are they here if they got what they wanted?'

'Love it!' muttered his granddad, as he walked back to the house.

'Well, think about the taxi firm. What if some drivers wanted to run it themselves and others wanted it to stay how it was, with uncle Jim in charge? What would happen?' his dad pressed.

'Why would they not want to?' his son persisted.

'Well, because people are all different and think different things, some might be happy with the way things are and not want them to change. Which is what happened in Northern Ireland.'

'What?'

'Not everybody wanted to be independent from Britain. Some wanted to stay part of the UK.'

'Why?'

'Oh, many reasons. Some thought that it would be better for them and for Ireland if they stayed. And because there was a big division in what people wanted and believed, it led to violence.'

'But why can't they just talk about it and come up with something that makes everybody happy?' said the boy.

'Because people sometimes believe things so strongly that if anyone disagrees with them, they get angry – which can very often turn to violence.

The little boy stood lost in thought.

'I know it's hard to understand.'

'I don't get why people would hurt each other for thinking different things. Isn't that what freedom is?' said the little boy.

His father looked at him and smiled.

'OK. What if I said that I believe that the sky is red and not blue – what would you say?'

'But it IS blue. You can see it's blue.'

'But what if to me it looks red?'

'Daaad, it's blue!'

'To you maybe it is – but what if the way I saw it was red? And, by the way, it IS red.'

'NO IT'S NOT, IT'S BLUE, DONT BE SILLY!' The boy boiled up with frustration.

'You see. See how easy it is to get angry at someone who doesn't believe the same thing as you, even though you know for sure that you're right and they are wrong.'

* * *

A few years later, at the start of a new century, a young soldier was walking back to his barrack block from the vehicle hangars – the same route that had been walked by generations of his country's soldiers. They had been in this country since the end of the last world war… which had ended nearly sixty years before.

He thought of the night ahead. Shower, change, phone home, telly, bed. He was skint, so going to the NAAFI was out – besides, it was a school night and he had PT in the morning. As he rounded the corner and approached the block, he saw two of his comrades stood outside chatting.

'Hiya mate,' one of them called.

'Have you heard the news?' said the other.

'No, what?' said the young soldier.

'Someone's flew a plane into the Pentagon!'

'Yeah, right. OK.'

'I'm serious. It's all over the news. BFBS, and all the German channels.'

'Really?'

'Yeah mate – check it out. It's fucking madness.'

The young soldier wasn't sure if his mates were taking the piss – playing a joke at his expense. He entered the block and made his way to the three-man room he shared with one other soldier. It was nice having a big room – lots of space. Every time someone new arrived they hoped that they wouldn't be put in with them.

As he approached the room he noticed the door was open and an excessive amount of noise was coming from inside. He went in and was greeted with the sight of bodies sitting around everywhere – on the couch, on the beds… on his bed.

'What the fuck?' he started.

'Jesus, mate! You wanna see this shit! Look!' His room-mate pointed at the large TV they had bought between them. On the screen were two tall buildings in what looked like New York. One of them was smoking as if a bomb had gone off on the upper floors.

'This a film?' asked the young soldier.

'No mate – this is the news! A fucking plane went into it!'

'What?'

'Yeah, someone has flown into the World Trade Centre in New York!'

'And the Pentagon!' someone piped up.

'What – by accident, or on purpose?'

'Don't know yet. They reckon it could be terrorists,' said his room-mate.

The young solider moved one of the lounging bodies from his couch and sat down. His room-mate passed him a can of lager from the mini-fridge

'This is madness mate,' his room-mate continued.

'Were there people on the planes?'

'Looks like it, yeah.' someone answered.

'Jesus!' said the young soldier, taking a large swig from the can.

'FUCKING HELL!' someone shouted.'

JESUS CHRIST!' someone added.

On the TV a plane had flashed across the screen and flown into the other tower.

'Did you see that?'

'This is crazy. What's going on?'

The whole room went into stasis; everyone was transfixed by what was unfolding on the screen and by the news announcer's words. The screen went from showing live footage and then back to the TV studio... back to Washington... back to the two towers. It seemed like one big loop.

'All those people...' said the soldier

As he said it, they saw a body fall from one of the towers.

'Bloody hell!' his room-mate exploded. 'Why would anyone do this?'

'I don't know mate.'

Without warning, one of the towers fell to earth. The room went silent. The whole world went silent.

'How... how many people were in there, do you think?' someone said.

'God knows.'

'Pack your bags boys. We're going to war,' said the young soldier.

'You think so?'

'I know so. This is… is massive. And we're gonna go to war over it.'

'With who?' his room-mate queried.

'I don't know – but the yanks are gonna go ballistic.'

'Jesus.'

They heard shouting and banging coming from the corridor. The duty NCO burst in the room.

'RIGHT LADS, I NEED THREE BODIES FOR GUARD DUTY!'

Everyone in the room shrank back into the wall. No-one wanted to volunteer.

'Three? Why three?' asked the young solider.

'They've put the alert state up to 'bikini black special'. Which means we have to double the guard.

A hushed whisper spread across the room. Everyone knew what that meant. Bikini black special was the highest state of alert in the armed forces, and they put it up for two reasons. One, the UK was at war and two, an attack was imminent.

'Come on lads, I need volunteers, don't make me pick people.' said the NCO.

'Sorry corporal, but we've been drinking,' the soldier's room-mate said –and waved his can of lager in the air.

'Right, OK. Her Majesty's armed forces around the world and the whole of NATO, have been placed on high alert and an extended state of readiness – and you cunts decide to get pissed.'

He left the room, knowing that he couldn't do a thing. No-one had done anything wrong.

'Prick,' someone said.

'Jesus! Look at that!'

The second tower fell.

'You think we are going to war, then?' his room-mate said.

'This is history. We are living through history. This is going to be one of them days when you remember exactly where you were, like JFK being shot, or princess Di dying.' said the soldier.

'How many people do you think have died?' someone mused.

'It must be thousands – the size of them buildings, the Pentagon, the fucking planes…'

'Who did it?'

'Don't know.'

'Some evil fucks.'

They sat watching the events unfold on screen. People came and went and came back again.

'Gotta give the cunts some credit, though,' his room-mate said.

'What do you mean?' the young soldier asked.

'Well, it's so simple. Just nick a plane and fly it into a building. BOOM! You've got absolute chaos and panic.'

'I know, mate.'

'What do you think will happen?' his room-mate asked.

'I've told you. War. And this won't be like Kosovo or Bosnia or Northern Ireland. I mean full-on, proper war. For real.'

His room-mate took a long drink.

'Well, here's to war then,' he said and held out his can. The young soldier hit it with his can.

'To war.'

* * *

Five months later the young soldier and his room-mate were in the vehicle hangars, working on one of the weapon systems. The cold January air flowed through the open shutters.

'I still can't figure the euro,' his room-mate said.

'Jesus it's not hard – just convert it to pounds'

'But it's confusing, I still work it out on the mark – that was easy. Three mark to the pound.'

'Well, convert euro to mark, then to pound – and you know how much things cost.'

'Nightmare that, though. Don't see why we need the euro anyway. I hope we never get it.'

'I don't think we will,' said the soldier.'

'I can't believe it's 2002 already. Don't seem like two minutes ago since the millennium.'

'I know, time flies.'

'How long the boss and sarge gonna be, do you think?' his room-mate asked.

'Not sure. Depends on how long the general keeps them and what he's got to say,' said the soldier.

'Notice how he doesn't want to speak to us mushrooms, though. Typical.'

'There's a reason we're called mushrooms.'

They looked at each other.

'Kept in the dark and fed on shit,' they said in unison.

'Look, here they come,' said the young soldier. The officers and senior NCOs came into the hangar.

'Get everyone in the cage,' said the sergeant. The men of their platoon gathered in the troop cage, which was where they kept the tools, equipment and spare parts. It also served as a de facto office and break room with old sofas and chairs.

The soldiers sat down and waited to hear what their leaders had to say. It wasn't every day a general came to the barracks. Something must be going on.

'Right, lads. I know your all dying to hear what was said at the briefing,' said the sergeant.

'Basically,' said the young lieutenant, 'you can aim off for being in the desert next January.' No one said a word. Every man sat and waited.

'Barring a miracle, and some major diplomatic skill, we will be finishing the job they should have done in '91,' the sergeant said.

'Now, we have a full training year to get through, but I want you to consider every exercise the real thing – because it soon will be,' added the officer.

The rumours had started a few weeks ago, fuelled by events on the news and the on-going war on terror. First it was Afghanistan. It seemed that the Americans wanted to rid the world of tyranny and terror ... to keep people safe.

'Any questions?' asked the sergeant. No one spoke.

Now attention would be turned to Iraq. They left the cage having been given some information that, compared to the first bombshell, didn't seem that important.

After the day's work was done, the young soldier and his room-mate walked back to the barrack block.

'This is fucking bullshit,' said his room-mate.
'What?'

'Iraq. It's bullshit. Ministry of Defence – not **off**ence!'

'We're soldiers – we don't pick the wars,' said the soldier.

'War on terror! How is invading a country 3,000 miles away gonna help keep my family safe?'

'There must be a reason – they must know something. Otherwise they wouldn't send us, would they?' said the soldier.

* * *

Months passed, and after a long and protracted period of failed diplomacy, the young solider found himself in a foreign land – at war with an enemy he didn't understand. The mission was to liberate the people from tyranny. And, in turn, it would keep his home and family safe.

He looked out from his sentry position. On the horizon the night sky was flashing and the faint sound of bombs and artillery could be heard in the distance.

The devastation was immense... as was the body count.

He was proud of being soldier. It was what he always wanted – to serve his country – but he couldn't help but wonder how any of this would help keep his loved ones safe.

* * *

From prehistoric man through to the modern combat soldier, the inhabitants of the planet earth had killed and maimed each other. Divisions between mankind fostered hatred and bigotry – race, colour, creed, language, nationality, politics, gender, sexual orientation and religion. All had divided humanity, since the very beginning.

The belief in a divine power was a tradition dating back to earliest recorded history – a belief that there is reason and meaning to life and that something that comes after, whatever that may be, have been the foundation of human endeavour. Now in the 21st Century, even with humanity's immense well of knowledge, there were still more believers across the globe than the faithless, despite the scientific facts that tested people's faith to the limit. After thousands of years, man's search for a divine force to explain the very reasons we exist hadn't ceased. And if there was a divine influence at work, such as the Abrahamic God, what would he make of his greatest creation?

If there was a god, what would he make of mankind's folly? All the wars, all the suffering and the hate. Would there ever come a day when he would say 'enough is, enough'? … and intervene on our behalf...

2

London, England... now

The bomb was almost ready. He needed just a few minutes more. He had been waiting for this moment forever.

Soon they would pay. The infidels would be punished for their sin. He placed the lid on to the plastic container holding the explosives, as gently as if it had been the arm of a newborn baby.

It was finished – and it was nearly time. Only a few things left to do.

He got up, went into the living room and opened up the laptop on the coffee table.

When it had finished loading, he clicked on the internet symbol on his home screen. He typed in the name of his email-provider and clicked 'go'. Logging into the email account, he couldn't help but smile. There it was, in the draft folder. Here was his final instruction. It contained only one word: 'Proceed'.

He deleted the email and shut down the computer.

Most people were not aware of how al-Qaida operatives received their instructions. Mobile phones were too easy to trace, but an email account on a public server was harder to link to the user. Everyone in the cell had the username and password for one email account on Yahoo or MSN. Their superiors would issue orders via email – but instead of sending them, they would save messages in the draft folder, and the operatives would log in to read them. And because no email was sent, it was virtually impossible to trace. There must be millions, if not billions, of email accounts worldwide – how could the authorities possibly track them all? Where would they even start?

He looked around his darkened surroundings; this apartment had been his home for the past four months, and he hated it. For Khalid, this place represented everything he hated about the west – the opulence, the luxury… the hypocrisy. The building he was in was designed to be the most exclusive address in London. The tallest building in Europe, it towered over the ancient metropolis, a twenty-first-century citadel of glass and steel. It was supposed to be a place for the wealthy and affluent – the great and good.

It stood above this once great city; a symbol of man's aspirations and ingenuity. It was pathetic – a futile gesture of self-importance.

So what, Khalid thought to himself, you have the tallest skyscraper in Europe. You used to have the largest empire in history. You were masters of all and feared no one. Then you gave it all up without so much as a scuffle and made way for a new empire – America. You became America's lapdog, a puppet nation, and the fifty-first state. You embraced their whole culture, Starbucks, McDonalds, Google and the absolute arrogance of believing your way of life superior, and that the only acceptable way of life was freedom and democracy. You also followed them in their ignorant crusade against Islam – even to the point of invading other countries. Some habits die hard don't they?

But how many peoples and nations would it be OK to trample on and exploit to make sure the all powerful stock markets didn't lose value and that your precious freedom was preserved?

Khalid hated America, but he despised Britain. He loathed the snivelling weaklings they had become. His grandfather had a misplaced respect for the British and said that they were honourable and fair, but also strong and powerful. As a boy Khalid believed this – but no longer.

Khalid got up and walked over to the floor-to-ceiling windows that were so popular in the city. He lit a cigarette and as he looked down at the cesspit of sin and debauchery below, he thought of how his imam had taught him the true nature of the West and of Allah.

It was just after Khalid had finished school that a man came to the mosque to preach about true Islam and the evils of the West. Khalid had never heard anyone speak the truth in that way before. From then on he pledged his life to Allah and to fighting 'the Infidel'.

It was not long before he was given a great mission. He was to become a martyr and take his place in paradise. He would kill the infidel and do Allah's will, but first he had to become one of them – blend in and not cause any suspicion. He shaved off his beard and started to wear western clothing, and came to Britain on a student visa. He studied at a college that was no more than a room above a shop – it was so easy, they didn't even bother to check, and when he started to look for a base where no-one would bother him from which to plan his attack, the infidels themselves helped him in his quest.

Shortly after he arrived in Britain, the country was plunged into the worst recession for a generation – the housing market crashed and rents dropped dramatically – which was how Khalid had ended up at Four Freedoms Tower – this shining beacon of 21st Century Britain. They were so desperate to rent out the apartments that they would take anyone – even a foreign student such as Khalid. The company that owned the building didn't even bother to vet him or ask how a student who did not work could afford to live alone in such an expensive two-bedroom apartment. All they cared about was that he paid the rent on time every month. So, for the past four months he had kept to himself. He didn't cause any trouble and he even managed to smile at the concierge on reception on the way in.

It was the perfect place to hide, among the wealthy – and those who pretended to be. It was the last place the authorities would think to look for a terrorist. But soon they would pay for their arrogance and sin.

Khalid dropped his cigarette on the polished hardwood floor and trod it out with his shoe. He then returned to the kitchen table and his preparations for his journey to paradise. There was still one thing left to do. He went into the bathroom to prepare – the prophet said that cleanliness is half of faith. 'There is no god but god, and Mohammed is his prophet,' he said.

He stripped down and began the purification process. He washed his face, nose, ears and mouth and ran his wet hands over his hair. Then he washed his right arm, including his elbow, then his left. He washed his feet and ankles and repeated the process three times before he could begin.

He put on the traditional loose-fitting dress, went back into the living room and placed his prayer mat in front of the window that faced the sacred house. That was the first thing he had made sure of when he took the apartment.

He raised his hands level with his ears, fingers apart but not spaced or together and said 'God is Great'. He placed his right hand over the left on his chest and looked at the place of prostration without lowering his head.

'O Allah! I declare you far removed from and above all imperfection, and that you deserve all praise. Blessed is your name. Your majesty (glory and might) is exalted. And there is no true god worthy of worship except you.' he said.

He paused for a moment and continued in a low voice. 'I seek refuge with Allah from Satan, the outcast. In the name of Allah, the Most Beneficent, the Most Merciful, I begin. In the name of God, the Lord of Mercy, the Giver of Mercy! Praise belongs to God, Lord of the Worlds, the Lord of Mercy, the Giver of Mercy,

Master of the Day of Judgment. It is you we worship: it is you we ask for help. Guide us to the straight path – the path of those you have blessed; those who incur no anger and who have not gone astray,' he continued.

'God is great,' he repeated, as he bowed down again, his hands on his knees. Grabbing them with his elbow, he made sure his back was straight and his head level with his back, as he had been taught.

'Far removed from every imperfection is my Lord, the Great. Far removed from every imperfection is my Lord, the Great,' he repeated twice more. He raised himself up, lifting his hands level with his ears.

'Allah hears the one who praises Him.'

Standing upright, he continued, 'Oh, our Lord! All praise is due to you.'

He reached the ground with his hands first and then his knees. 'Allah is the Greater.'

He rested on his palms and placed his forehead, nose, knees, and feet on the floor with his belly away from his thighs, his toes erect, arms away from the ground. He intoned, 'Far removed is my Lord, the Most High, from any imperfection,' and repeated it twice more, then raised his head. 'God is great,' he added.

He sat up on his left leg, keeping his right foot upright, and put his hands on his knees.

'Oh, my Lord, forgive me.' He rested on his palms again as before. 'Far removed is my Lord, the Most High, from any imperfection' – and having repeated it twice more, raised his head, then again, 'God is great'.

He stood up and began again. Again, his hands positioned as before, he intoned, 'God is great'.

Again, with his right hand over the left on his chest, and looking at the place of prostration, head high, he continued.

'O Allah! I declare you far removed from and above all imperfection, and that you deserve all praise. Blessed is your name. Your majesty (glory and might) is exalted. And there is no true god worthy of worship except you.'

He paused for a moment, then continued in a low voice, 'I seek refuge with Allah from Satan, the outcast.' Then again, 'God is great,' as he bowed down, as he had been taught. Again he repeated, three times, 'Far removed from every imperfection is my Lord, the Great, and raising himself up, his hands level with his ears, 'Allah hears the one who praises Him.'

Once more he stood upright. 'Oh our Lord! All the praise is due to you.' Reaching down to the ground first with his hands, then his knees, 'Allah is the Greater', and again assumed the prostrate kneeling position before continuing, three times, 'Far removed is my Lord, the Most High, from any Imperfection'.

He raised his head, 'God is great,' then sat up on his left leg, his right foot upright with his hands on his knees. 'O, my lord, forgive me.'

He knelt, resting on his palms again to repeat, three times more, 'Far removed is my lord, the Most High, from any Imperfection,' before raising his head. 'God is great,' then stood up.

He sat down again and held his right hand closed, his thumb and middle finger touching to make a circle and pointed his index finger down. 'All compliments [Allah is free of all imperfection, His is the dominion, Magnificence, Endless existence belongs to Him], prayers, and pure words and deeds, are due to Allah. May Allah grant the Prophet safety from all defects and imperfections and keep his message safe from all evil; may Allah grant him mercy and honour. May safety and security be granted to us and to all the righteous slaves of Allah. I bear witness that none has the right to be worshipped except Allah, and I bear witness that Muhammad is His slave and Messenger,' moving his finger as he spoke.

'Oh Allah! Praise Muhammad, and on the family of Muhammad, as you praised Ibrahim, and the family of Ibrahim. You are indeed worthy of praise, full of glory. And send blessings on

Muhammad, and on the family of Muhammad, as you sent blessings on Ibrahim, and the family of Ibrahim; you are indeed worthy of praise, full of glory.'

He resumed, 'Oh Allah! I seek refuge with you from the punishment of the grave and from the trail of Messiah, and from the trail of life and affliction of death. Oh Allah! I seek refuge with you from sins and from being in debt. And I ask you, Almighty God, be with me this day so I may fulfil my mission and enter your paradise.'

He turned his head to the right and said, 'May Allah's peace, mercy and blessings be upon you,' then turning to the left, 'My prayer is concluded. Prayer is concluded.'

He rose and rolled up his prayer mat before going into the kitchen to make a coffee. While he waited for the kettle to boil he lit a cigarette and contemplated what he was going to do that day. He would become a martyr and take his place in paradise. He would get his houri. Then his mind turned to death. What was it like? Would it be painful? Was he wrong? Stop it. Blasphemy!

He pushed the impure thoughts from his mind and took a long drag on his cigarette. The kafirs and infidels were blind in their ignorance. Why could they not see the glory and majesty of god? It made no difference now. Soon they would pay for their sins.

3

The alarm went off suddenly, shattering the quiet of the bedroom. Andy Baker hated that sound and everything it meant. It meant he had to move – open his eyes and get out of bed.

He reached out from under the nice warm duvet to grab his phone and shut it up. He considered turning over and going back to sweet oblivion, but he got up anyway. Today was an important day. He had a meeting in the city that, if it went well would earn him a lot of respect at work, not to mention a hefty bonus come Christmas.

Andy was in advertising and had been at the agency Cheetam and Grants for the past three years. He had just been promoted to 'Senior Account Executive', which meant he got all the big fish – the multinationals and the household names.

Andy didn't make up the ads – that was down to the creative team. It was Andy's job to sell their ideas to the client and manage the account from a business perspective. He had always been a good salesman; his boss Mike, a senior partner at the firm, said that he could sell sand to the Arabs or freedom to the Yanks. This was in part the reason for his promotion. The partners had put a lot of faith in Andy, sending him down to the capital to pitch for a major account.

He had always thought it strange that a big ad agency didn't have an office in London, but then it wasn't really a big firm in terms of people, however, in terms of turnover it was huge. Mike told him that it was a balance between prestige and financial prudence. To rent an office the same size as the one they had now would cost probably triple in London – then factor in rates and wages and the profits would start to dwindle.

Andy cradled his head in his hands then rubbed his eyes. God he was tired. He picked up his phone to check the time and found he had a text message. He opened up the text, which was from Tess, his wife. It read

'GOOD LUCK 2DAY SWTHART ME EN THA KIDS MIS U LOADS XXX LUV TESS XX'

Andy smiled at his wife's attempt at text-speak. She still thought she was twenty-one, although both of them were now the wrong side of thirty.

His mind drifted back to the last conversation he had with her, not twenty-four hours ago. It was teatime and he'd just got in from work, he got through the door, put his coat on the hook and placed his bag at the foot of the stairs, as he always did. He took out the two bags of buttons for the kids and made his way to the kitchen. Tess was cooking tea of beef stew and dumplings.

'Bloody hell, for a feminist you can't half cook!'

'What can I say? If we left it to you we'd be on a diet of beans on toast and potnoodles, unless you tried something exotic. Then we'd all get salmonella.'

He walked up behind and put his arms round her waist, gently kissing her on the neck. 'You had a good day?' he asked.

'Yeah, not bad. You?'

'Hectic – trying to get everything sorted for tomorrow.'

'What time's your train?'

'Quarter past seven. Should get into to Euston around half nine, and hey, they're only sending me first class!'

Taking his arms from Tess's waist, he put the buttons in a cupboard, as she got some more food out of the fridge.

'First class, eh? I knew I married you for a reason.'

'That you did.' Andy loosened his tie and went through the mail on the kitchen table.

'Oh, yeah, the council tax is overdue.'

'Why? It should have been paid, did it not go out of the account?'

'The direct debit stopped, remember,' she said. 'They took it before you got paid and it bounced.'

'That's so stupid. Why does it have to come out on the fifteenth? And of course the bloody council won't let you change when you pay, oh no!' he grumbled.

'Pay it on the credit card,' said Tess.

'Yeah, I can do. Not the point though, is it?'

'So, first class. You **are** going up in the world Mr Baker.

'Ha ha. Yeah, I know – never been in first class in my life. I hope the drinks aren't too expensive.'

'It's all complementary. You get a meal, too.'

'Really?'

'Yeah, you muppet. It's all free.'

'Well, thank you very much, Mr Branson,' said Andy. 'Where're the kids?'

'Upstairs, playing on Jake's air hockey. Did you get the 'Shake and vac'?'

'Aw, sorry, I forgot.'

'Andy! The one thing I ask you to do. I wanted to do the stairs before my mum and dad come at the weekend.'

'Why? What's wrong with them?'

'Nothing – but you know what my mum's like.'

'I don't get it. Why is it every time they come we have to blitz the house top to bottom? It's not as if it's a pigsty. We don't do it for **my** mum and dad.'

'Don't start. You know my mum – she'll be looking everything up and down and finding fault everywhere.'

'So, they're supposed to be coming to see you and the kids, not inspecting the house.'

'I know, but I just feel better knowing everywhere is spick and spam.'

Andy flicked through the rest of the mail – all bills. Gas, electric, water, phone, credit card, store card, mortgage.

He caught something out of the corner of his eye in the back garden.

'LOOK! LOOK! IT'S BLOODY CATFACE!' he called.

Tess joined him at the window. 'Where?' she asked.

'There at the bottom of the garden – Catface!'

In the back garden, the neighbour's cat was sniffing around. The same cat that sneaked through the back door in summer and stole food that had been left on the side.

'Look at him, cheeky bastard! Mooching around, cool as you like,' said Andy.

Tess laughed. 'Don't let it bother you – it's just a cat.'

'Well, it's our garden, and it can't just come in and do whatever the hell it likes. Look! Oh, DON'T DO THAT!' Andy shouted, as he banged on the window. The cat didn't move. It just stared at them.

'Dirty bastard!' Andy said. Tess laughed and went back to cooking tea.

'You and that bloody cat – or Catface, as you call it.'

'Yeah, have you seen it? It's got a real catface.'

'Well, it being a cat, you'd have thought so.'

'No, I mean, some cats are cute and have cute little fluffy faces, but that – that is a real cat face, like an Ancient Egyptian drawing. It's evil! Beady little eyes staring at you.'

They heard a banging noise make its way down stairs. 'Here they come,' said Tess.

'MUUUM! JAKE'S CHEATING!

'NO I'M NOT. SHE'S JUST RUBBISH!'

'OK, calm down. You can both come down now – tea's nearly ready.'

'Hello,' said Andy. His children smiled at him. 'Come here and gives us a hug.' He held his children close. 'OK, who wants to see some magic?' he asked.

'Oh yeah!' said Maggie.

'Real magic, dad?' asked Jake.

'Yes, real magic! Now, wait for it.' He clapped his hands and then clicked his fingers five times. 'Have a look in the sweetie cupboard.'

Jake and Maggie opened up the cupboard where they kept the treats, sweets, chocolate and crisps.

'You magicked us buttons!' Jake crowed.

'Yeah, I did!'

'Mum, mum! Dad magicked us some buttons!'

'Did he, now?' said Tess. 'Well, you can have them after tea.'

'Aw.'

'**AFTER** tea,' Tess insisted.

Andy smiled as Jake and Maggie went into the living room to watch TV.

'They'll figure it out eventually, you know. You won't be able to fool them for ever,' said Tess.

'I know – but I love the look on their faces.'

'Mmm. So, what time d'you think you'll be back tomorrow?' said Tess.

'I'm gonna leave immediately after the meeting, so I should be back mid-afternoon.'

'Well, don't forget it's Jakes assembly tomorrow. The school got in touch – seems he's getting an award.'

'Is he? That's brilliant.'

'Yeah – they said we can go and watch.'

'Fantastic! What do you want to do – should we meet there?'

'Depends on what time you get back. I might be able to pick you up.'

'OK, I'll ring you when I'm at the station.'

Now, in London, in the firm's apartment, Andy sat up in bed. He smiled to himself as he thought about his wife. They had met while studying at university – she was reading English and Journalism and he was doing Business and Marketing. From the moment he saw her, he knew she was the one. His mates thought he was soppy and took the piss out of how loved up he was. But it had been nine years, five of them married, and they were still going strong. Andy thought about how lucky he was – he had everything any man could want – a beautiful wife, two great kids… the only thing missing was the money. He'd never really wanted to be rich – just secure. If he could pay off his mortgage before he turned fifty, he'd be happy. A nice comfortable life was what he wanted – and that his children were happy. That was the most important thing to him – his kids. Jake would be seven next month and Maggie nearly four.

The best part of Andy's day was coming home from work and being greeted by Superman and Snow White, or whatever costume they were wearing that day, and hearing them tell him about what they'd been doing,

but despite the love and affection Andy felt towards his wife and children, love alone would not pay the bills. He and Tess struggled financially once Jake was born – they were still quite young and Tess wanted to be a full-time Mum, which left Andy as the sole breadwinner. He didn't mind – deep down he preferred the old-fashioned family unit. It wasn't that he was a chauvinist – if Tess wanted to go back to work he would have supported her one hundred per cent. But she didn't. She wanted to be a mother first and foremost, and the thought of strangers – a nanny or child-minder – looking after her son made her uncomfortable. He agreed with her. He felt that a child should have at least one parent around all the time.

Things had got better over time, but when Jake started school and Tess was about to return to work full time, they had discovered that she was pregnant again. Although they were in a better position than when Jake was born, another member of the family would certainly eat up the small disposable income they had. Andy had not really wanted another child – the thought of doing it all over again with the nappies, the sleepless nights and everything else. But then the thought of abortion made Tess's blood run cold. Andy didn't think of a foetus as a person – not that early on anyway – but he went along with Tess; the thought of losing her was too bitter to contemplate.

So for nine months he had gone round in a daze, worrying about how they would cope – not just financially, but emotionally. How would Jake feel? He'd had their undivided attention all his life – would he be jealous? How would Andy treat his new child? Would he love it as much as he loved Jake?

All that changed the moment he met his daughter. When the nurse passed him a little bundle of blankets containing Maggie, an overwhelming flood of pure love and affection washed over him, and he knew from that moment just as when Jake was born, that he would do anything – absolutely anything – beg, borrow, steal and even lay down his own life or take another, to make sure his children were happy and safe.

He got off the bed and switched on the apartment lights, the sudden brightness forcing him to squint as his eyes adjusted. He still couldn't get over how nice this place was – the furniture alone probably cost more than what he made in a year. God alone knew how much the rent was, but Mike said the accountants had done their homework and renting a high-end property such as this was still cheaper than putting up everyone from the firm who came to London in a hotel. Plus it was tax deductible – even with all their money, the partners were still a bunch of tight-fisted old goats.

Andy walked over to the en-suite bathroom but paused to take in the magnificent view from the window. There below him, spread out in all its majesty, was London. So much history had happened here, from the plague to the Blitz. Today though, the City of London would play host to another historic event – the biggest deal of Andrew Baker's career.

He got his wash-bag out of his case and went into the bathroom. God, it was nice. One day he'd have a bathroom like this of his own. He ran the hot and cold taps and filled the basin with water – not too hot, not too cold. He splashed water on his face to wake himself up and began the morning ritual.

He sprayed a dollop of shaving foam into the palm of his hand and rubbed his hands together and began to massage the cream over the lower half of his face, cheeks, chin, and neck, running his finger over his top lip. He fitted a new blade on his razor – a Gillette 'Mach 3 Fusion'. Five blades. He had used the same brand ever since he started shaving – it was what his dad had used and he had yet to find a better or closer shave. Even the traditional barber's shop shave he had in Turkey didn't really come close. When he had first started to shave, Gillette made only three-blade razors, but then they brought out one with four, and now five.

He dipped the head of the razor into the water and glided it along his cheek in an upward movement. Up first, five times. He put the head back into the water to remove excess foam and began to work down his cheek. Down again. Five times – the way his dad had showed him. The chin was next, then top lip, followed by his neck. Up five times, down five times.

Then wash away all the foam, wash his face, then into the shower.

Freshly showered, he returned to the basin and cleaned his teeth, wiping the mirror where the shower had steamed it up. In the bedroom he began to get dressed. His suit was hanging out, ready. There was something about wearing a nice suit – the feel of it – that appealed to him. He put his socks and boxers on first, as always. Then his shirt and trousers – size thirty-four. It didn't seem two minutes ago that he wore a thirty… how times change. Still, that was the harbinger of the inevitable. The onset of middle age was just around the corner.

Next his chosen tie, then the hair wax. He rubbed between his hands and worked it through his hair. He was lucky – some of his friends were losing theirs. With his jacket on the morning ritual was over. Now he was ready to face whatever the day had in store. The child inside always felt like Batman when he got dressed for work – suiting up for battle. He laughed at himself for even thinking it. You watch to many cartoons with Jake.

He caught a glimpse of himself in the mirror; you know what, mate? Not bad, not bad at all. Today is going to be fantastic. Knock 'em dead at the meeting, and then home in time for Jake's assembly. Nothing can stop you now.

4

Khalid fastened the rucksack holding the bomb. He was ready. He checked the apartment one last time to make sure there was no evidence that would lead the authorities back to his friends.

He stepped outside the apartment and, locking the door behind him, put the keys in his pocket – even though he would no longer need them. Force of habit, he thought to himself as he made his way down the corridor and round the corner to the lifts.

As he summoned the lift, felt a wave of nervous anticipation and that feeling in the pit of his stomach his mother used to call butterflies. He watched the digital display above the lift as if it was doing more than just counting up the floors – 44, 45, 46, 47, 48. Khalid shifted his posture slightly to prepare for his transport's arrival – 49, 50, PING! The lift doors opened, filling the empty corridor with an unnatural glow.

He stepped into this new environment of designer glass and marble, pushed the fat 'zero' button that was slightly bigger than the rest, and as it lit up the doors closed behind him. He stared at the now locked doors and could not help but smile – in a few minutes and he would be on his way to the train station, and in less than two hours he would meet Allah in paradise and be rewarded for his courage.

For all the technology and weapons at their disposal, the infidels could not stop him or his brothers from destroying them. They had no weapon capable of defeating their cause and right now, no power on earth could stop Khalid from entering paradise.

* * *

Andy quickly scanned the apartment one last time to make sure he had everything – wallet, phone, keys. He put his overnight bag in the hallway so when he came back later he could just pick it up and be straight out. He thought about taking it with him, but it might look as if he was in a rush and wasn't focused on the meeting. Besides, he had a couple of hours to waste after the meeting before his train was due.

He turned off the lights, locked the door and walked to the lifts.

He had such butterflies. God, he was nervous – but also excited. If he pulled this off… he stopped himself from thinking about the best outcome. His dad always told him hope for the best and plan for the worst. All he could do was do his best and knock them for six.

He pressed the button to summon the lift and waited anxiously for it to arrive. Reaching into his coat pocket, he pulled out the silver case Tess had bought him for Christmas and took out one of his new business cards. They were a lot flashier than his old ones, and he smiled to himself as he read his name and title. Everything was coming together and he really felt that nothing could stop him know.

The digital display above him showed 49, 48, 47, 46. Strange, Andy thought, it was coming down and not up. He wondered who else was up and about at this ungodly hour. Then 45, 44, PING! The lift doors opened and Andy was taken aback – someone else was in the lift.

'Morning,' he nodded to his new companion as the lift doors closed behind him. He was about to reach for the ground floor button, but it was already lit up. The young man next to Andy just nodded his head in brief acknowledgement of his presence.

Chapter 4

Andy hated these awkward social situations – he never knew quite what to do, left alone with strangers on the train or in a waiting room. Should he make polite conversation or just pretend they weren't there? He didn't want to appear ignorant – but then he didn't want to come across as some weirdo who talked too much, like when people give you that look as if you're from another planet just because you said that **you** liked reading Harry Potter too.

He took a quick glance at the young man standing in the lift next to him – he was carrying a rucksack and looked like a student – young, scruffy – but these days you could never tell.

As the lift descended, Andy's ears popped, and he opened his mouth like a goldfish a couple of times. It was a little trick his dad had taught him and he always used it whenever he flew. He didn't really want to think of how fast they must be going for his ears to pop – if Tess were here she'd be terrified. She'd always had a phobia about lifts and enclosed spaces, and whenever they were alone together in a lift, Andy would jump up and down to try and make it stop – which it never did, but he found it amusing to see her squirm. It was revenge for all the times she'd thrown the top of a tomato at him and pretend it was a spider. He hated spiders – horrible things. Tess and the kids would roar with laughter when he jumped out his skin and his voice went up a notch whenever he found one.

Suddenly Andy was plunged into darkness and nearly knocked off his feet as the lift came to an abrupt halt. A split second later the lights came back on – not as bright as before, but he could still see. Andy took a few seconds to compose himself, then looked at the young man with the rucksack who was also seemed panicked by the sudden halt.

'Wonderful, absolutely wonderful.' Andy said. This had better not take long, he thought, as he looked on the panel for the emergency button to call for help. 'Of all the days,' he said, pushing the call button.

The intercom crackled to life and a disembodied voice asked, 'Hello, can you hear me? Is everyone all right?' Andy leaned down to talk into the intercom. Who was this designed for anyway – why put the speaker so low? 'Yes, yes we are OK. There's only two of us.' He took a quick glance at his companion as he waited for a reply.

'OK sir, this is the concierge from downstairs. I am going to call an engineer out. I will get back to you as soon as I have an ETA.'

'What, is there no override or anything?' Bloody excellent, he thought. He'd got up early so he'd have time to prepare, but now he could be late for the meeting anyway.

'I'm afraid not, sir. Standard procedure is to call out an engineer. I'll call back when I have news. Just sit tight.'

The intercom went silent, leaving Andy and the young man alone.

'Great,' he sighed to himself, as he leaned against the lift wall opposite Khalid. He took a moment and considered this young man – perhaps now would be an appropriate time for small talk, so he held out his hand to him. 'Well, it looks like we're in here for bit. I'm Andy.' The young man's handshake was limp.

'Khalid,' he said, and continued to stare into space.

Clearly this was going to be a long morning. 'So, you off on holiday?' Andy ventured, in the vain hope of more than a one-word response.

'Something like that,' he replied, without meeting Andy's eyes.

Andy was briefly taken back to the family holiday in Portugal last year.

'God, I wish I was going away. Last holiday we had was paradise, absolute paradise'.

Khalid looked at Andy for the first time.

'So, where you off to?' he pursued, but before Khalid could answer the intercom crackled to life.

'Hello, can you hear me?'

Andy put his head back down to the mouthpiece. 'Yes we can hear you fine. What's the news?'

'The engineer said he's going to be about two hours,' said the concierge.

'Two hours! Is this some sort of a joke' Andy screamed into the mouthpiece. 'Look, I've got a really big meeting to get to and the lad with me has a plane to catch,' he said hoping that this would make a difference. 'Is there nothing else that can be done?'

'Sorry sir, afraid not. Is there someone I can contact for you?'

Andy calmed down smiled to himself. No one would be up at this time anyway, and even if they were, what could they do? He felt a little guilty at loosing his temper – after all, the man was just doing his job. It wasn't his fault the lift had stopped. 'No, not at this ungodly hour, thank you'.

'OK sir, I will get back to you when I have more news.' Andy turned to Khalid and realised he had forgotten about him, 'Sorry, do you want him to call someone? Have you a taxi booked or anything?'

Andy's companion shook his head and became very agitated. Checking his watch, he began to mumble in a language Andy didn't understand. He tried to calm him down. 'Hey its all right. I'm sure the engineer will be here in less than two hours. They always say it will take longer – it makes them look good when they get here in twenty minutes.' Andy continued, not sure whom he was trying to convince. He didn't need to be stuck here with this lunatic.

Without warning Khalid put the rucksack on the floor and shouted in English, 'Shut up! Shut up, you annoying fool!' He turned away from Andy and gently placed the rucksack in the corner of the lift. 'Need to think. Need to think,' he muttered to himself, as Andy quietly moved away from him into the opposite corner of the lift.

Andy wanted to do something to calm him down. 'Look, I'm er sorry if I upset you, but I'm sure the airline or holiday firm will understand if...' but before he could finish Khalid interrupted him and started talking to the wall.

'It's over. I have failed. All for nothing ... all for nothing.' Khalid slid down the wall to a sitting position and cradled his head in his palms.

Andy was beginning to feel alarmed at this behaviour, but there was nothing he could do but stare at him in wide-eyed disbelief. What could he do? He was stuck here with this guy, so he slowly stepped over to him and gently placed a hand on his shoulder. 'Hey it's all righ…

Suddenly he found himself being pushed up against the wall and knocked off balance so he could do nothing but slump into the corner, and when he looked up, he was staring at the barrel of a handgun. Andy's heart stopped for a moment, but then began beating at a thousand beats per minute. His world turned a funny shade of sepia, but at the same time every detail seemed magnified a thousand fold.

'Keep your pig mouth shut, or I will put a bullet in your fucking head,' Khalid snapped, gesturing with the gun. Powerless, Andy instinctively raised his arms to protect his face and began to cower and shake. He had never been so scared. The closest he had ever come to a gun in real life was the armed police at the airport, but this was terrifying.

'Oh Jesus, please, please don't hurt me,' he pleaded as Khalid stood over him, stared down at him like a boot over an ant. The rage in his eyes briefly disappeared.

'The false idol you people worship will not help you now, infidel.' Khalid took a step back, and with the gun still pointed at Andy's head he opened up his rucksack and unclipped a cable from the bomb. Andy saw the contents of the rucksack and plucked up the courage to speak.

' Is… is that a…a… bomb?'

'Yes,' Khalid replied, as coolly as if Andy had asked him if it was raining.

'Why do you have a bomb?'

The rage came back to Khalid's eyes. 'Because I am a holy warrior of Islam, and I am meant to kill the infidel in the name of Allah.'

Andy could only sit, dumbfounded and confused. He couldn't begin to contemplate what this young man was saying, and like a child stating the obvious, the only response he could muster was, 'You… you're a Muslim?'

'Yes Andy, I'm a Muslim.' A look of satisfaction spread across the young mans face.

'You look shocked, my friend. Is it because I'm white?'

5

Khalid could not help smiling at Andy's ignorance. He was a typical example of the cretinous West; they all had a ridiculous notion that their enemy had dark skin. If only they new the truth – that Islam and the teachings of Mohammed were universal and transcended petty issues such as language, citizenship and the colour of people's skin.

In a former life, Khalid went by the name of Josef Reiniger. He was born in Hamburg, Germany to a typical middle class family – a workaholic father, an unfaithful mother and a grandfather who dreamed of the redundant and long lost ideology of his youth. He was born into a world on the precipice of the digital age, and by the time Khalid had reached double figures, the internet, mobile phones and globalisation reigned supreme. Mankind had built machines that could observe the farthest reaches of the universe and the tiniest subatomic particle.

But the one thing that overshadowed all these advances in mankind's technological progress during Khalid's short life – the thing that one day historians would come to consider as defining the early twenty-first century was, ironically, man's oldest pastime. War. However, this was not a war between two nations – this was a war of ideologies, fought between the brave warriors of an ancient and sacred brotherhood and the ignorant sinners of the capitalist west, who had ruled and ruined this planet for far too long.

And now Khalid would do his duty, for his brothers, for Mohammed and for Allah.

Once upon a time Khalid didn't believe in a supreme being. Like most of his generation, music, movies and the 'World Wide Web' became his places of worship. Then one day the world changed. In the space of a few short hours the status quo had been knocked out of balance for ever. From that moment, there was only the world before and the world after. Khalid was only a boy at the time, but that afternoon was engraved on his memory like a brand from the Almighty himself.

The eleventh of September, two thousand and one. The day of the opening salvo of the war on terror – that was what the infidels called it. Terror to them maybe – but now, to Khalid it was a glorious victory… one that Khalid hoped to emulate. But first he had to get out of this lift. It must be a test from Allah to prove he was worthy, he thought, as he watched Andy glancing from the call button on the panel back to the pistol pointed at his head.

'Don't even think it,' he said. The infidel could not even look at him. Good, he thought as he sat down in the corner beside his rucksack.

Khalid watched Andy in quiet contemplation, and couldn't help being reminded of his grandfather – the old solider who couldn't come to terms with defeat, until he saw an opportunity in the form off his only grandson to carry on his ridiculous dogma.

The boy who would become Khalid spent a lot of his growing up time with him. His parents had to work during school holidays, so he would be shipped off to Bavaria to be indoctrinated into National Socialism. For hours, the old man lectured the boy, pontificating on events long past and dreaming of the day when the *Reich* would be returned to glory. The old man would never see his dream come to pass. One morning,

Josef went downstairs for breakfast and found his grandfather slumped in a chair.

At first Josef thought he was playing a trick – was this another lesson? Why was his skin so pale and waxy? Josef quietly stepped over to him and realised something was wrong, he placed a finger on his cheek and the cold from it spread throughout his young body, sending him recoiling across the room to find the nearest place of safety.

He didn't dare move from behind the sofa – he did not want to look at the terrifying form in the chair. It felt like an eternity before the housekeeper arrived and let herself in, and it was only when the boy heard her scream that he moved from his hiding place.

The hours and days that followed were just a blur to him now – he could barely remember the funeral. Of course, his parents insisted that he have counselling with a therapist, so for a while he did. Josef went back to being a normal boy and spent his formative years like most of his generation, browsing the internet, social networking, listening to music and watching movies.

But Josef became bored and frustrated with modern life; he didn't see the point of it all. His whole life was laid out in front him – when he finished his education he would get a job, maybe one of many, he would get married, maybe have children and then die. A pointless and pathetic existence.

Then he met Kareem, a Turkish immigrant whose family ran a local takeaway that Josef frequented with his friends.

His grandfather's influence made Khalid wary at first, but over time he warmed to Kareem and the two became close friends. It was Kareem who introduced him to Islam and showed him that there was more to life than the pitiful ways of the infidel and the corrupt greed of the West. He changed his name and embraced Islam with every fibre of his being, spending hours immersed in the Qur'an and the works of great scholars. He watched 'the war on terror' from afar, but soon came to realise that the cause of Al Qaida and the Taliban was just.

He thought of going to the front to fight with his brothers, but a preacher at the mosque told him that Allah had greater things for him to accomplish and set him on the path that led him here, to this moment. This was a trial from above, he was sure of it. He could not – must not – fail now.

'Are you scared, Andy?' he asked the infidel, who could still not look up.

'Yes,' came the reply, in a strained, terrified whisper.

Khalid was going to enjoy this. 'Do you know what I was planning to do?' he asked. 'I was supposed to get on a packed train and when it was well on its way,' he lovingly patted the top of his rucksack, 'do my duty for Allah and Islam and take my place in paradise.'

On hearing this, Andy finally looked at the monster. He was repulsed and disgusted at this man – he had a thousand things he wanted to say, a million questions to ask – but the one at the forefront of his mind was simply, 'Why?'

Anger and surprise spread across Khalid's face. 'Why? Why? What do you mean "why?" Because it is Allah's will.'

'Killing yourself and murdering innocent people?' Andy said.

'It is not murder – it is jihad – holy war, and you are my enemy,' Khalid shouted, his voice loaded with anger and contempt.

A terrible silence descended on the lift, broken a few moments later by the intercom crackling to life, startling both men.

'Hello, sir, sir can you hear me?'

For a brief second both men did nothing, then Andy jumped for the intercom. It was a desperate move, but he had to get out of there. 'Help, Jesus help, he's got a guu...' his words were stopped short by the cold, evil barrel of

Khalid's pistol pressing into the back of his skull.

'No, no, my friend' Khalid whispered as he manoeuvred Andy away from the intercom and turned him round so the pistol was pointed between his eyes. Andy began to get that familiar feeling in the back of his throat, his eyes started to water and he involuntary started to sob. Khalid smiled and put his finger to his lips. 'Shhh!'

'Hello sir, I didn't catch that, you were breaking up. Is everything all right?' the concierge said.

'Yes, everything is fine, my friend here is a little panicky. He doesn't like small spaces,' said Khalid.

'Well, you're both perfectly safe. We'll have you out of there in no time. Just sit tight. If you tell him to sit down, it will help him to breathe.'

'Ok I will, thank you' Khalid said before turning to Andy. He gestured for him to sit with the pistol. 'You heard the man. Just sit tight.'

6

'Just sit tight Josef, we're almost there.' said his father. The man who now called himself Khalid had retreated into the dark recesses of his mind. His name was Josef and he was eight years old.

Josef was sat in the back of his father's car on the way to see a head doctor. Since his grandfather had died, his parents had booked to take him every week, and this was his second time. Josef felt sick in cars – he always had.

His father parked outside the office where the doctor worked and escorted Josef inside. His father checked in with the lady at the desk and they sat down in the waiting room. They sat in silence as his father read a magazine. It wasn't long before the doctor came out and called Josef's name. His father got up and spoke to the doctor – a nice lady who always asked him strange questions. Josef couldn't hear what they were saying, but then, 'Josef, you go with the doctor. I'll be here when you done,' and his father sat down again.

'OK.' Josef looked at the lady doctor who smiled at him. 'How are you Josef?'

'I'm well, thank you,' he replied.

'Come on in then. I want to hear everything you've been up to since we last talked,' she said as they walked into her office. The office was nice – very bright, with nice paintings on the walls and some toys in the corner.

'Take a seat Josef,' said the doctor, sitting down opposite him. They made themselves comfortable on the bright red beanbags. The doctor picked up a notepad and pen as she did the time before. 'Right then, let's begin. So, how's school?'

'It's fine.'

'And what have you been learning about?'

'We've been learning about plants this week'

'And do you like learning about plants?

Josef thought about it. He wasn't sure. 'I don't know. It's OK, I guess.'

The doctor wrote something on her pad. 'You said last week that your favourite subject was history.'

'It is.'

'What do you like about it?' she asked.

'You have to know about history so you don't repeat the mistakes of the past,' he replied. For a few moments the doctor didn't say anything. She stared at him, then wrote something down.

'Who told you that Josef? Was it your teacher?'

'No.'

'Then who?'

'It was something my grandfather used to say,' he said.

'Did you spend a lot of time with him?' she pursued.

'I did, I stayed with him during the holidays. I told you last week.'

'Yes, yes you did. My mistake. Did he tell you a lot of things?'

'Yes.'

'How do you feel when you think about him?'

'I feel sad.'

'Why is that?'

'I didn't say goodbye to him,' he said, as she made some more notes.

'Would you like to? If you could see him and say goodbye, would that make you feel better?'

Josef thought about it. 'Yes, maybe.'

'I ask because your father told me that his funeral is in a few days, and if you want you can go and see him in the funeral home – if it wouldn't upset you too much. How would you feel about that?'

'You mean his body? Going to see his body?' he asked, incredulous

'Yes.'

Josef remembered the day his grandfather died and how scared he was, in that room, alone. 'Would I have to do it on my own?' he asked.

'No, not if you don't want to. I'm sure your mother or father would be with you.'

'I think I'd like to,' he said. 'Then I can say goodbye.'

The doctor wrote something down and smiled at him. 'OK then.' She continued, 'While we're talking about you grandfather, what other things did he tell you?'

'He told me about history and about the war.'

'What did he tell you about the war?'

Josef shrugged his shoulders, 'Lots of things.'

'Like what?'

'That if we had won, the world would be a better place.'

'Did he ever say how or why the world would be a better place?' The doctor was scribbling notes on her pad.

'He used to say the world wouldn't have the problems it did if the *Reich* was in power.'

'Did he now?' the doctor mused. Josef got the feeling that the shed didn't agree.

The questions continued for ages and Josef answered them all. She asked more about his grandfather, what he did in the war and what Josef felt about it all, and what he thought.

'OK, Josef. Time's up for this week. Well done. Thank you.' The doctor got up and led him outside to the waiting room, where his father rose and spoke to the doctor again, but Josef didn't hear what they said. Outside, at the car, his father asked, 'How are you feeling, Josef?'

'I'm OK.' His father nodded and drove off. 'Good.' They wove through the busy streets until they got on the *Autobahn*. Neither Josef nor his father spoke. Josef stared out of the window and thought about his grandfather. 'Never tell anyone what we speak of,' he used to say. And Josef didn't. He had told the doctor very little about his lessons and nothing of the Jews or the Communists.

'So, Josef,' his father said, breaking his daydream, 'would you like to go and see you grandfather?'

'I would… if it's OK,' Josef replied. His father smiled at him through the rear-view mirror.

'Of course it is. We'll go tomorrow if you want.'

'OK,' said Josef.

His father drove on in silence, leaving Josef with his thoughts. They had moved his grandfather's body up from Bavaria to bury him here, to be near the rest of the family and Josef's grandmother, who had died before he was born.

They came off the *Autobahn* and headed for home. Most of the journey had been in silence. His father parked on the drive of their house, a large detached residence in a nice suburb. 'Home again,' said his father.

Josef saw that his mother's car wasn't there – she must be out shopping he concluded as they went into the house. It was nearly teatime and the sun was going down. 'Right, Josef, I need to catch up on some work. Why don't you go and play in your room? Mum will be home soon,' said his father.

'OK.' Josef went upstairs and his father went into his study. Josef turned on his computer and played games until he heard his mother's car pull on to the drive. Josef paused his game and went downstairs, where he heard his parents talking loudly at each other in the kitchen.

'NO! He's eight years old. Hasn't he been through enough?' His mother sounded angry.

'It's what he wants. He wants to say goodbye to my father properly. And my old man would want it,' said his father.

'I don't give a shit what that monster would have wanted.'

'Hey! He wasn't perfect but he was still my father and Josef's grandfather. He wasn't that much of a monster when we needed him to look after Josef was he?'

'Well, if I'd known what…'

'Don't give me that! You knew what my father was and what he did in the war – and what he believed,' said his father as Josef walked in.

'What's going on?' His parents went quiet and looked at each other.

'Hello sweetheart,' said his mother, giving him a hug and a kiss. 'We're just talking about what went on today. You know you don't have to do anything you don't want to.'

'I know mum,' he said. 'But I do want to go and see granddad, so I can say goodbye.'

His father gave his mother a look that said, 'see, told you so'. 'OK. As long as you're happy about it.'

'I am,' he said, as she gave him another hug.

Josef set the table while his mother prepared dinner and his father went back to his study, only coming out when the food had been served. They ate dinner together, and when he'd finished Josef asked if he could be excused and play in his room.

'Of course, sweetheart.' His mother put her hand on his and squeezed it. As usual, he went back to his room, where he would stay until one of his parents, usually his mother, came up to tell him to go to bed. Josef didn't care all that much – he preferred his own company anyway.

He opened a drawer in his computer desk and pulled out his grandfather's last gift – a hunting knife that bore the symbol of Aryan supremacy. He removed it from its leather sheath and felt the cold metal between his fingers, caressing every inch of it as he studied every detail. His parents had no idea he had it, but it was all he had from his grandfather. The old man's possessions had been boxed up and put in storage or simply thrown away. He gently kissed the knife's handle and put it back in its sheath and shut it in the drawer.

Josef turned on his television and flicked through the channels, and caught the end of a programme and following that, a trailer for the next program – a film. It was *Schindler's List*, and he had heard about it briefly from his grandfather. It was about a traitor to the *Reich* and full of lies and Jewish propaganda, he said. Josef decided he would watch it.

While the adverts were on he got undressed and put on his pyjamas. He made himself comfortable on his bed ready for the film to start. Then, for nearly two hours, he watched transfixed by the events it portrayed. He barely heard his mother coming up the stairs, and he turned off the television just as his mother entered his room. 'Time for bed, Josef,' she said, a little surprised that he was already in his pyjamas. 'What have you been doing?' she asked.

'Just reading,' he lied.

'You're so clever.' She kissed him goodnight and tucked him in. 'Good night, darling,' she said when she got to door. She turned off the light and stood in the doorway. 'I love you, Josef.'

'I love you too. Good night.'

His mother closed the door, leaving him in darkness. He listened to her footsteps going down the stairs and when he was sure she was gone, he pulled out the remote control which he had hidden under his pillow and switched the television back on, turning the volume down so his parents couldn't hear. He'd only missed a little bit of the film and he was quickly immersed in it again. Towards the end of the film, Josef watched the man called Schindler say goodbye to the Jews on his list. They gave him a ring they had made from some teeth. He collapsed against his car and began to cry, saying that he could have saved more.

Suddenly Josef's world came crashing down, and he began so sob uncontrollably. He couldn't see for the tears – could scarcely breath. Sadness turned to despair. Despair transformed into rage. He turned over and buried his head in his pillow. He let out a muffled cry of pain and banged his fists against the bed.

When he had calmed down, he turned off the television and dropped the remote on the floor. He tried to go to sleep but the tears and sobs carried on until finally, his young mind and body gave in to tiredness and he fell into a deep, dreamless sleep.

The next morning his mother woke him. It was a Saturday, the sun was shining – but he could tell it was cold outside. He washed and dressed then went downstairs for breakfast. His father was at the kitchen table reading the newspaper. 'Good morning, Josef.'

'Morning, father.' His mother prepared him a bowl of cereal that he ate in silence. His mother drank coffee and his father continued reading.

'Are we still going to see granddad today?'

His father lowered the paper and stared at the boy, 'If you still want to.'

'I do.'

His mother got up and left the table, kissing Josef on the cheek as she went.

An hour later Josef and his father were in the car on their way to the funeral home. Most of the journey was spent in silence as Josef stared out the window, like he always did. He thought about what he was about to do. Would be scared like he was before, or would he be OK? He thought about what he would say to his grandfather.

They arrived at the funeral home and before they went in Josef's father asked him again if he was sure he wanted to do this. Josef was sure. They went in and told the man at reception that they were there to see his grandfather. The man led them to a room full of chairs. It was a smaller version of a church, but instead of an altar there was a coffin with the lid off – in which lay his grandfather. The man left Josef and his father alone.

They walked down the long aisle towards the coffin, which grew larger with each step. Finally at the side of the casket, Josef looked in upon the face of the old man with whom he had spent so much time. He looked peaceful – as if he was sleeping.

Josef felt his father's hands on his shoulders. 'He's in a better place now, son.' Josef said nothing. He stared in silence at the old man – he looked different, as if it wasn't him, but a copy of him.

'Can I have some time alone, father?'

'Are you sure?' His father tried to hide his surprise. 'Will you be all right on your own?'

'I will,' said Josef. 'I'll be OK.'

'I'll be right outside if you need me,' said his father, squeezing Josef's shoulders lightly as he turned and left. Josef heard his father close the heavy door. He was all alone with the body of his grandfather and he stared again at the old man, taking in his pale, waxy skin and gaunt face. He turned his head to make sure he really was alone.

'You left me.' he said. 'You promised you would always be around. You told me that the Jews were evil. You said we should have won the war. You said National Socialism was the only way the human race could survive.' He leaned his head towards his grandfather's and said bitterly, 'You lied to me. You lied. You lied about all of it. And now I'm alone. You've left me alone – with them,' he continued. 'Why? Why did you do that? Why did you lie and why have you left me alone?' Josef's anger and rage boiled to the surface. 'Answer me! Answer me, old man!'

Josef brought his fist down hard on the old man's chest. 'Answer me!' he repeated, as he hit him again. 'You lied!' Another impact. 'You lied to me,' he raged as he pounded his fists on the corpse of his grandfather. 'You were one of the bad guys!' Another punch. Josef hadn't even noticed that he'd been crying, and now he took a step back and composed himself. He wiped away the tears.

He stepped back to the coffin and leaned in, his face next to his grandfather's. 'You lied to me all my life, and now you've left me alone with them. I hope you burn in hell. Good bye.' Josef turned away from the coffin and paused momentarily before making his way out. He had noticed something out of the corner of his eye, and he turned his head to look at it. It was a large statue of Christ, positioned so he seemed to be watching over the coffin – guarding it somehow. Josef stared at the lifeless image of mankind's saviour. 'You've caused more death than anyone,' he thought as he neared the door. He found his father waiting outside.

'Are you OK, Josef?' His father gave him a rare hug.

'I'm OK.'

Getting down on one knee, he wiped the tears from Josef's face. 'It's all right son. I know you. I know. Come on, let's go home.'

Josef's mother was waiting for them, and as soon as the car pulled on to the drive she rushed out to make sure Josef was OK. With a hug and a kiss, she ushered him inside, then Josef went into the living room and watched cartoons. He could hear his parents arguing in the kitchen – probably over him. Eventually, his mother came in with a drink.

'Here you go, sweetheart.' She sat down next to him on the sofa. 'Are you OK, darling?'

'I'm fine.'

'If you ever want to talk, you know I'm here.'

'I know, mum.'

His mother hugged him – the type of hug only a mother can give, that said everything would be all right and there was nothing to be scared of. Suddenly all Josef's pain and emotion came flooding to the surface, and he cried and cried.

'Shush now, angel. It's all right. I'm here,' his mother whispered. They stayed, clinging together on the sofa for what seemed like ages. He felt safe there – loved. He put behind him the things he felt when he was with his grandfather – the old man, the old solider, the Nazi – a man whose whole belief system rested on the notion that the colour of his skin and the country where he was born made him innately superior to everyone else on the planet.

A few days after Josef visited his grandfather's body, he went to his funeral. It was not well attended – there were a dozen people at the most. Josef's father had requested that his medals be buried with him.

It took Josef a long time and many sessions with the head doctor to regain his mental calm, but the shadow of the old man never left him completely. He immersed himself in the history of the Second World War, the Nazi party and Hitler's rise to power.

He learned that when a nation feels downtrodden and betrayed, when all hope seems lost and apathy and ignorance has taken hold of its soul, the people will turn to anyone or anything that promises to restore their sense of worth. To Josef's young mind it was very simple. Hitler's rise to power was not a master class in leadership, political insight or military prowess. It was simple psychology and intuition. He told the people what they wanted to hear, with passion and emotion. He felt the pulse of the nation and acted accordingly. The German people had been defeated in the Great War and had spent more than a decade in darkness. They wanted their pride and dignity back, and all Hitler did was say he could give it to them – although he didn't say how. By the time everyone realised how he meant to achieve it, it was too late. They'd gone too far down the path and there was no turning back.

If the powers that be let the people down often enough, if the major mechanisms of civilised society such as politics, democracy, finance, business and the media break down and oppress the people often enough, and if at every turn people see only injustice, poverty, crime and social decay, there will come a time when the people will say, 'enough is enough'. They will follow anyone who tells them things can be different. That was how Hitler rose to power – and that was how he could cause the deaths of over twenty million people. This is how all monsters gain power – by taking advantage of vulnerable people, then giving them what they want… or what they tell them they want.

The process starts with the discrediting of everything that stands in their way – political freedom, the press, and the economic system. They make people believe none of these can be trusted, or are fit for purpose. They make people believe that they have no control of their lives, that one person cannot ever make a difference – that the system in place is too large and too corrupt. They create an enemy– something to be feared, and something different – something no one fully understands. Then the monsters blame this enemy for all society's ills. For a long time the people do nothing and carry on as normal. After all, no one likes change – it has to be done slowly. Then, when the people are downtrodden enough; when they have been browbeaten enough; when they are sick and tired of being let down at every turn by the very things that should exist to serve them, that's when the monsters appear. But they never look like monsters – they appear as saviours who can make things better – lower taxes, cut crime, make the military strong and the economy vibrant, and do all the things that an average citizen wants – or has been made to believe that this is what they want. The people fall for it every time, hook, line and sinker. Caesar, Napoleon, Stalin, Hitler, Mussolini. They had all gained power by the same means. After all, the greatest feat Lucifer ever achieved was convincing mankind he didn't exist. People are strange.

Despite his youth, all this seemed glaringly obvious to Josef. History repeated itself over and over again. Society became corrupt and decadent, the people became downtrodden, while those in power and the elite became complacent, arrogant, convinced of their superiority and secure in their positions. Then a monster would appear and take over, and it would take a war and countless deaths to stop them. Afterwards, when the dust has settled, the cycle starts again.

There had to be something more – something more than this endless, mindless circle. During the course of his therapy, Josef found out he had very high intelligence. It became more of a curse than a blessing. He could see the patterns and cycles in human nature and history.

By the time he was ten years old Josef had outshone all his classmates – but this made him lonely and made him question everything. It didn't help that his relationship with his parents became increasingly dysfunctional. His father retreated into his work while his mother found other pursuits. The only solace Josef found was reading, and he read books on all subjects, becoming a sponge for knowledge.

But this knowledge wasn't enough. He wanted more... needed more. He felt that there had to be something more. One day Josef started to read *The Bible*. At first it was hard to understand – the language and the structure. At school they talked of God and Jesus, but Josef however didn't believe a word of it. At the tender age of ten, he could see flaws in the dogma and ideology. From the very first page, *The Bible* contradicted science – in the beginning God created heaven and earth... only he didn't, because scientific fact had proven beyond doubt the age of the planet earth and the time of 'the Big Bang'. Science had also proved the existence of the dinosaurs – which were never mentioned in any religious text. The more Josef, the more he disbelieved. If God existed, why did he allow his so-called greatest creation to make so many mistakes, including the crucifixion of his only son? What was 'heaven'? Where was it? What was hell? If Lucifer was a fallen angel, how could he have become as powerful as God? According to religious teachings, the modern world was full of sin – sex before marriage, sodomy, war, famine, disease. In modern society, the Ten Commandments were broken on a daily basis by millions of people around the globe. And what happens when you die? If you have been good you go to heaven ... and if you've been bad you go to hell. How many souls were in existence? What about animals? Weren't we all God's creatures? Do dogs and cats have a soul? Do they go to heaven? What about the fish in the ocean and the birds in the sky? Do they all have souls, or was it all a lie – a fairy tale to give meaning to pointlessness? A way to control the teeming masses?

To Josef, religion had no place in the modern world. The celebrations and festivals had become nothing more than a joke – a way to make money. Easter and Christmas had all lost their religious significance a long time ago, and to Josef the modern world was full of hypocrisy and contradictions. It was a long time before he found his place in the world and a meaning to his life.

He eventually found that meaning in the form of Allah and Islam, which jolted Josef from the torpor of modern existence. When the truth was revealed to him, it was as if a great weight had been lifted from his shoulders. Life had meaning and purpose – and that purpose was Allah. The boy called was Josef was reborn as the man Khalid. He had travelled a path that had led him here – to this time and this place – London, England. He had been given a great mission in the name of Allah and of Islam, but now he was being tested – he was sure of it. Now here he was, trapped inside this little box – with the infidel. Why had this happened? Khalid hadn't even considered that the lift might fail – it never entered his mind – and now he found himself alone with his enemy.

'You heard the man. Just sit tight,' he heard himself say. He felt the gun in his hand, pointed at the infidel. He felt powerful and in control. He could put a bullet in this man's head and no one would know until they reached the ground. Then what? How would he explain it? What would he do? Would he run? No. That would cause alarm and panic. The authorities would come looking for him. Nothing must get in the way of his mission.

Khalid contemplated the man sitting opposite him. Who was he? Who was this 'Andy'? What did he do? Did he have a family? Friends? Should he shoot him right now? All these things whirled through his mind as he tried to formulate a plan of action. From a sense of control, he now had a strange feeling of helplessness. For so long he had known what he was going to do – he had a plan and he would follow it through. But now his plan had hit a snag. He had never once thought that he would be delayed on his way to the target. His mind had always focused on the act itself – on detonating the bomb, and on how it would feel. What would it be like to be incinerated, to have his body liquefy from the shockwave of the bomb? Then there was what would come after – paradise, meeting Muhammad and getting his reward. Eternal peace.

Khalid didn't know what to do. If he shot this man who shared the lift with him he would have to run when they got to the ground floor. If he did nothing, there was a good chance he would be caught before he could accomplish his mission. There must be another option – there had to be – but what?

He decided he would wait. Maybe if he did nothing, the infidel would be too scared to do anything. But what would happen when the lift was fixed? The anticipation and anxiety were too confusing, so he would do nothing and wait, and see what happened.

7

The concierge turned away from the intercom panel at the side of the lift in the lobby and made his way back to the reception desk. This was all he needed – a bloody claustrophobic and a foreigner stuck in the lift. It had been such a quiet night with nothing going on – and now this. It was sod's law, the bloody lift going down right at the tail end of his shift.

He walked round behind the large, shoulder height reception desk, and sat down. Once again he phoned the on-call engineer to get an update. The automated system started its spiel. Why real people couldn't answer the phone anymore was anyone's guess. As he waited, he gazed round the award-winning foyer of Four Freedoms Tower, with its post-modernist design of marble, metal and wood. It was a nice environment to work in – 'aesthetically pleasing' was what the jumped-up little facilities manager called it, pretentious prick that he was. Just because he had letters after his name, he thought it gave him carte blanche to look down his nose and talk down to people as if they were children.

All the same, it could be worse, he mused. He could be looking after a building site instead, sitting in a port-a-cabin all night freezing his family jewels off. His thoughts were interrupted by the woman on the other end of the phone, in some far-flung dump that probably didn't even have lifts.

'Hello, hi I called before about a lift being stuck at Four Freedoms Tower… Yes, that's the one, I just wanted to know roughly how long the engineer is gonna be…' She started making excuses.

'I understand that, but I've got two blokes stuck in there and one of them is starting to panic – plus people are gonna be getting up soon and there will be hell to pay if all the lifts aren't working.' He took a deep breath and looked up at the ceiling as she put him on hold – so she could call a man thousands of miles away from where she was, to ask him how long it was going him to get to a location that was probably less than ten miles from where he was sitting, on hold. What a ridiculous concept, he thought, as he listened sullenly to the stupid music these companies used when keeping you on hold, in the mistaken belief that it would take your mind off the boredom of waiting. The fatuous music just reinforced his contempt for the modern world, and how the big companies treated people like so many sheep and numbers.

He hated the hypocrisy. Why advertise that you provide great customer service and treat people as individuals when you clearly don't give a rat's arse, pigeon-holing people in to demographics and groups. Yes – the customer is always right – until they can't pay or need some help with the product or service they provide. Then they send them round the houses to every department, putting them on hold every five minutes, grinding you down until you slam the phone down in frustration – and then have to start the process all over again.

At last the far-away voice came back and told him what he needed to know. 'OK, right. Thanks for your help,' as he put the phone down and returning to his crossword, he had forty minutes before the engineer turned up. Bob Fitzpatrick had enjoyed doing crosswords for years now – he'd started doing them on his breaks at the car plant over thirty years ago. He'd started on the factory floor when he was twenty years old and had worked his way up to shift supervisor. Then, after being there thirty years, the company announced that they were shutting the plant and moving operations abroad because it was cheaper and the advances in technology meant that a computer could do the work of a hundred men.

Bob had been devastated, as if he had lost a family member, and in a way he had. Men and women he'd seen every day for years, close friends and colleagues – not to be seen again. All the birthdays they had celebrated together, the Christmas parties and nights out – all over. He felt as if his life was finished, and that he had wasted the best part of it. Bob simply couldn't understand the company's logic – why spend all that money to build a new plant, half way round the world, to build cars that would be driven by the people in the country that their current plant was in? Because computers could do it better and this was the way forward – free markets, globalisation and all the other nonsense that was bandied about at the time. It just made him bitter.

As for the government, they just sat on their backsides and let it all happen, and now industry and manufacturing had been decimated, and a way of life destroyed that could never be restored. And it was all because of money. The companies wanted more profit and the automated, computer-controlled robots that replaced Bob could give them that.

Soon computers were running everything – but they still broke down and malfunctioned – which meant that an entire industry had to be built up around them. 'Information technology' – young men in cheap suits going about with an unearned sense of their own importance – their 'I-know-things-you-don't-know' attitude made Bob sick.

The irony of it all was that every minute of every day, somewhere a computer malfunctioned, proving that they weren't so great after all.

Bob had become very bitter about the plant's closure and began to regret having spent so much of his life there. The only consolation was that it was at the plant that he had met his 'husband', Jimmy. Bob had known, right from being a teenager, that he was gay – but back then it was still illegal, so he had had to keep it hidden from his family and friends. He had led a double life, sneaking out to certain pubs on his own and having one-night-stands with men twice his age.

Then, at the plant, he had met Jimmy – the love of his life, his soul mate. They had been together nearly thirty years and when civil partnerships were recognised, they had been first in the line. It was a big moment for them – even though homosexuality had been made legal a long time ago, it felt at last that their love had been recognised the same way as everyone else's was. They had always known that the love they felt for each other was no different from if they had been 'straight'. Now here they were, an old married couple, arguing over what to watch on the telly. Thank God for Sky +, Bob thought, or they might end up in divorce court, fighting for custody of the dogs.

It had been Jimmy who persuaded Bob to go back to work instead of moping round the house and wasting his redundancy money on expensive holidays and home improvements. The problem was that either he wasn't qualified for most of the jobs available, or the interviewers thought he was too old. Then he came across an advert in the paper for a night watchman. He didn't mind shift work, although twelve hours was a bit much – but he took it anyway. It wasn't mentally or physically challenging work – in fact it was more boring than anything else.

He had only taken the job to avoid being bored at home, and at first he only did a couple of shifts a week to tide him over. Then ten years ago the security company he worked for was bought up, and the new owners offered him another site. It seemed he had impressed them somehow, because the new post paid a lot more than his old one – a real plus when recession had hit them hard.

On the strength of long service he was offered a plum position at 'Four Freedoms Tower. The place had only been open a few months, and as usual the builders did not have everything done in time, so for the first few weeks no one lived there. When the residents finally started to move in, they were all wealthy and very polite and kind – after all, Bob knew how to charm people – he always had done. But the honeymoon didn't last long, because the housing market crashed and not only had the apartments lost their value, but the owners could no longer afford to be selective about their new tenants. They would let to anyone daft enough to pay the still expensive rents they were asking.

Soon the building was full of bloody students, immigrants, drug dealers, conmen and all kinds of scumbags who lived shoulder to shoulder with the millionaire businessmen, footballers, actors, doctors and barristers. Bob's job quickly became very weird, as the building evolved into a melting pot of all sections of modern society.

The owners had run out of money before the building was finished, so they had to skimp on some vital systems – such as the lifts. A building of Four Freedom's size had only four lifts, which were of course, controlled by a computer. The other lads on the team were convinced that the computer was female and had menstrual cycles, causing the system to break down at least once a month. However, Bob was sixty-two and far too long in the tooth to let it bother him.

He finished the last clues of his crosswords and returned to his home page. He quickly scanned the news section before logging into a social networking site Jimmy had showed him. A couple of Christmases ago, Jimmy had bought him a laptop for work and a dongle so he could use the internet. Now Bob was addicted to the internet – all the knowledge in the world in one place; whatever you wanted to know was at your fingertips.

He would while away the tedious hours on his shift, downloading music to his mp3 player, watching films, contacting friends old and new – and he was getting paid for it.

He checked the time on his watch. God it was going slowly. Roll on seven, he thought.

8

Inside the lift, Andy and Khalid sat in opposite corners, more like prize-fighters in a ring than two men waiting to be rescued from accidental incarceration.

It was Khalid who broke the silence. 'I should be in paradise – should be with my houri. I should be being celebrated by my brothers as a martyr,' as he turned his head to the wall.

After a few moments Andy finally found his voice, 'Do you really believe that?' he asked carefully. He was still in shock to find that the man sitting just a few feet from him was a would-be suicide bomber.

'Of course,' Khalid began, scornfully. 'It is the way of Allah – something your kind will never understand … which is why you must be purged from the earth.' His every word dripped hatred.

Andy considered this, a million thoughts echoing round his head. He was sure that Khalid wouldn't shoot him. If that was what he had wanted Andy would be dead already.

'What I do understand is that you want to kill hundreds of innocent people, most of who probably don't believe in ANY god, let alone one that would condone murder,' he said, surprised at his own logic. With a spark of confidence continued. 'What I really don't understand is why? Why would you want to do this? I mean, you're clearly not from a Muslim country, so why?' he demanded, staring at Khalid for the first time.

'Innocent?' Khalid said, ignoring Andy's question. 'Your armies are occupying Muslim lands; you pander to the will of the Americans. That is not innocence.'

To call this young man 'disturbed' would be an understatement of epic proportions, Andy thought as he tried to fathom Khalid out and think of a response. He decided to swallow his fear.

'So, because our government made some bad choices, we all deserve to die? For a religion we don't even believe in, so you can go to paradise? Bullshit!' As he said this last word, Andy realised he had gone to far, as a flash of anger spread across Khalid's face.

'You know nothing, ignorant pig. There is a global jihad against America and its allies; a fatwa has been issued against you and we will drive all non-Muslims from all the lands of Islam by any means and with maximum carnage, until we have caliphate and…'

'And that includes blowing yourself to bits,' Andy said, interrupting the obsessive rant. He knew enough about Islam to realise that this man was deluded. Andy had Muslim colleagues at work, and they told him that what al Qaida believed was just a different interpretation of the Qur'an, and one that the vast majority of Muslims disagreed with. He was intelligent enough to know that extremists came in every stripe, and al Qaida and the Taliban were no different from neo-Nazis or the Klu Klux Klan – they might be at opposite ends of the spectrum, but they all used hatred and violence to reinforce their opinions.

Khalid began to speak. 'Allah has bought from the believers their lives and their money in exchange for paradise. Thus, they fight in the cause of Allah, willing to kill and be killed. Such is his truthful pledge in the Torah, the gospel and the Qur'an – and who fulfils his pledge better than Allah? I shall rejoice in making such an exchange… this is the greatest triumph!' Khalid's eyes burned with a fire so fierce and his words were laced with so much hatred it made Andy want to creep away to a place of safety where this madman could not hurt him... but that was not an option. He had no weapons and no escape. All he had was himself.

'Look I'm not religious or anything,' he ventured. 'I was brought up a Christian, but I don't really believe in it. To be honest, God is low on my list of priorities. All I want is a good life for my family, a nice house, decent car, maybe holidays abroad – and make sure my kids don't go without. I work really hard so I can get these things. I don't break the law. I pay my taxes and all my other bills – and for what? For some stranger I know nothing about to kill me and leave my family devastated, over something that has nothing to do with me or the way I choose to live my life. I'm sorry, but from what little I know about religion, no god would condone murdering innocent people. You can believe whatever you want – that's your right – but don't come to my homeland and use violence to shove your beliefs down my throat.' Andy stopped and looked away from Khalid in disgust. He was quite proud of the way he had stood up to him. Maybe what he had said had got through to him?

'Andy, you don't understand. How could you? You're a godless heathen. You live in a corrupt and sinful culture. You turn a blind eye while your leaders wage war in Muslim lands. You're more concerned with tending your garden and watching American propaganda films, while your bombs drop on Muslim schools. That is why I am here. We are at war and it is the individual duty for every Muslim who can do it, in every country possible, to kill the Americans and their allies in order to liberate the holy mosques from their grip and to get their armies out of the lands of Islam – defeated and unable to threaten any Muslim. This is in accordance with the almighty Allah.'

Before Andy could formulate a response to this lofty rhetoric, Khalid continued, '… and to fight the pagans together as they fight together, and to fight them until there is no more tumult or oppression and justice and faith in Allah prevail.'

Andy felt the remaining colour drain from his face. He felt the acids in his stomach rising to the back of his throat… he was going to be sick.

He just managed to control himself and not vomit, but he could not stop his eyes from filling with tears. He started to sob quietly but uncontrollably.

9

Andy's sobbing stopped as, in his mind's eye, his wife started to breathe deeply. His memory had taken him back almost four years, and he was sitting, helpless, on his sofa at home, as his wife Tess was on all fours, trying to ease the pain of her contractions. It was the day they'd been waiting for so long – the day he would meet his daughter.

Nine months ago Tess had started to become distant. At first he thought it was just 'that time of the month' with the usual mood swings. One minute she would love him to bits, the next she would hate him and want to bury him in the garden. Then the moment came – the four words you never want to hear the person you love say: 'We need to talk.'

He'd come home from work and slipped into the usual routine of having tea, bathing Jake and putting him to bed. Andy had read Jake a story and tucked him in, and had gone downstairs where he found Tess sitting, staring morosely on the sofa.

'What's up with you?'

'Andy, sit down. We need to talk.'

'OK.' He sat down beside her and prepared himself for the worst. She was leaving him. Had she met someone else? His heart beat faster and those all-too-familiar butterflies entered his belly. Andy loved Tess with every atom of his being. He still found it hard to believe that a woman like Tess could ever love him – she was so far out of his league. Andy knew this all too well, and was always ready for the day when the penny dropped and she realised it as well.

'What's up?' he ventured.

'Andy, I'm pregnant.' Tess looked him directly in the eye, the way women do when they want to know what a man is thinking. She found nothing.

'But when? How? You're pregnant? Are you sure?'

Tess reached into her bag and pulled out a pregnancy test with its little indicator stick.

'Take a look,' she said, passing Andy the stick.

Chapter 9

There in the little window was a plus sign, clear as day. Positive. He was going to be a father again. The flood of relief that Tess wasn't leaving him was quickly followed by a feeling that can be best described as, 'Shit!' They were having a baby... again.

'How far are you?' he asked.

'Six weeks or thereabouts.'

There was an awkward, uncomfortable silence as she waited for him to say something to give her an indication of how he felt. After what felt like a lifetime he smiled. 'That's wonderful.' He put his arms round her, held her close, smelled her hair.

'We're having a baby!' she laughed, and Andy could feel her happiness.

'We are!' He tried to echo her feelings, but deep down he had reservations. How were they going to afford another baby? They lived in a two-bed semi – where would the child sleep? How would Jake take it? Sleepless nights. Nappies. Bottles. Prams. Car seats. They'd have to do it all over again – Andy wasn't sure he really wanted that.

'We have a lot to talk about,' she pursued. And for the past nine months that was almost all they had talked about – the new baby and everything and anything related to it. Now though, today was the day.

In the early hours of the morning Tess had started to have minor contractions, but her waters still hadn't broken. That had been around 3 am, and it was now 10.30. Andy had googled 'how to bring on labour' and found a website, one of many that suggested ways that you could speed up the process. One of the suggestions was getting on all fours and rocking backwards and forwards – which was what Tess was now doing in the middle of the floor as Andy searched for other things to do.

'Ooooh, fucking hell that was a big one!' Tess gritted her teeth.

'Come on babe, your doing great. Remember to breathe.'

'Thanks for the advice you fucking idiot! 'Cos I forget to do that sometimes.'

Hormones. Living with a pregnant woman was a task in itself. You can be as supportive, loving and caring as you like, but then the hormones kick in and you're the anti-Christ.

There was a knock at the door and Tess's mother, Julie, came flying in. 'Oh my God, it's happening. It's today. Are you OK, sweetheart?' She took off her coat off and put her bag down.

Julie got down on her knees and started to rub Tess's back. 'It's OK darling, your doing great. Remember to breathe.'

'OK, mum,' Tess agreed.

Chapter 9

Julie got up with purpose. 'Right, Andy, have you phoned the hospital? We need to get her in,' she said.

'I have. They said not to come in until the contractions are two minutes long and thirty seconds apart.'

'That's bloody ridiculous. Didn't you tell them she was in pain?'

'I did, and they said to give her some painkillers and get her into a warm bath.'

'That's just stupid. It's nothing to do with health or medical reasons. It's 'cos they haven't enough beds. Bloody NHS.' As much as Andy's mother-in-law could be a pain, in this instance she was right. In the last couple of years the NHS had decided to save money and close the maternity unit at their local hospital. He doubted that the doctors and nurses agreed with it – it was more than likely that some pen-pushing bureaucrat had come up with a money-saving idea. 'I know, let's close some of the Trust's maternity units and just have three bigger ones across the city.' A city with a population of nearly three million people. The hospital where Jake had been born used to look after over 200,000 people on it's own, but now, when Tess was ready, they would have to drive right across the city to the nearest maternity unit. Bureaucracy had prevailed – yet again.

Andy's company had once had a contract with a local council. They had wanted to run a campaign encouraging people to vote, so Andy and the creative director met with them to discuss it. That day he found out why millions of people didn't vote. Plato once said that, 'The penalty for not engaging in politics is being governed by your inferiors'. And 'inferior' was the operative word. If the general public knew what kind of men and women actually ran things – important things that affected everyone's life – there would be riots and revolution.

Andy had never thought of himself as especially clever – he was bright and good at his job, but he was no Einstein. The day he met with the officials at the local authority he felt like the smartest man on the planet. It wasn't that they were stupid – although some of them obviously were – they were arrogant, out of touch and woefully ignorant about the people they claimed to work for – the public.

The council spent £250,000 on the ad campaign, so you would have expected the voter turn-out to have gone through the roof. But it didn't. And when they asked Andy what had gone wrong, he felt like saying, 'You people. You're what's wrong. You're the reason people don't vote.' But he didn't – he kept his mouth shut, which is where the problem really lies. If more people were aware of how things actually worked and got involved, maybe there would be decent people in charge. And maybe if more people did speak up, society wouldn't have some of the problems it had, and the bureaucrats and pen-pushers wouldn't be able to get away with closing maternity units.

'Arrrrgh... oooh, oooh. They're getting worse,' Tess gasped.

'Try standing up, love.' Julie helped Tess to her feet. Andy put a hand on her shoulder. 'Come on babe, you can do this. We'll be meeting Maggie soon.' He ran a loving finger across her face and smiled.

Maggie was the name they had chosen after a long debate and many vetoes about picking a name. At first they were in two minds about knowing the sex of their baby but as the twenty-week scan approached, they both decided that they did want to know. Besides, it would make it easier decorating the baby's new bedroom, buying clothes and all the other things a baby needs.

Soon after they knew Tess was pregnant, they had decided to convert the house to three-bedrooms by partitioning an area off their bedroom – and to Andy's surprise it actually worked. The house looked good and everyone had their own bedroom.

On the day of the scan, Andy left work, picked up Tess at home and they drove to the hospital.

'Are you nervous?' he asked, as he pulled up at a set of traffic lights.

'A little bit. Are you'?

'Little bit, yeah,' he said.

'What do you want it to be?' Andy thought about it as the lights changed and he drove off.

'I'm not bothered either way – just as long it's healthy,' he said firmly.

'If I'm honest about it, I think I want it to be a girl. I think that would be a nice way to complete the family… although I wouldn't be bothered if we had another boy as long as everything's all right.'

They pulled into the hospital car park and Andy went to get a ticket for paying on exit. He wondered how much money went to the hospital from parking fees – after all, thousands of cars must use this car park every week, but all the signs bore the logo of a private company that had the contract. He wondered how much profit they made from patients and visitors.

He helped Tess out of the car and they set off slowly towards the hospital. The car park was across the road and about 100 meters away from the main hospital building. As they headed for the maternity ward, doctors, nurses, porters and visitors milled around, going about their business. Andy couldn't help but notice that the actual medical staff – doctors and nurses – were significantly outnumbered by non-medical staff. They all wore official ID tags round their necks but no indication of what they actually did. Were they admin, office workers, receptionists, IT? He wondered if it was of any comfort or reassurance to the patients and visitors to know that, no matter what happened to them, the paperwork would get done and the computers would be? How did anyone ever survive going to hospital years ago, before there were computers, and thousands of management and admin staff? The NHS must've been a mess back then.

They rounded a corner and entered the quasi-maternity unit. The scans were done at this hospital, but the baby would be born on the other side of the city in a different hospital. Tess handed the young man at reception her paperwork for a twenty-week scan, which he processed and then told them to take a seat.

All around the waiting area there were other couples and pregnant women. A big forty-inch flat-screen TV was showing a 24-hour news channel, but Tess picked up one the many women's magazines from the coffee. Andy watched the TV, not really paying any attention to what was on. He heard the doors to the unit open and out of the corner of his eye he saw two women and a gaggle of children approach the reception. He, along with everyone else in the room, couldn't help but hear what they were saying.

'Ah'v cum for me scan,' said one of the women, who was probably in her early twenties. She was wearing a pink velour tracksuit, on which the waistband bore the legend 'sexy bitch' in gold italic lettering. The trousers hung low enough to reveal a tattoo on her lower back – what one of Andy's friends referred to as a 'tramp stamp'. From her appearance she was an aspiring 'wag' – too much make-up, badly applied fake tan, cheap hair extensions, false nails and thick black false eye lashes. She was heavily pregnant, however no-one in the waiting area was likely to be fooled into thinking that the father was a successful footballer.

Her companion, a young woman nearly three times her size and with a face even the Brothers Grimm couldn't have dreamed up, was trying, without success, to herd their children – one of them had thrown himself on the floor. She grabbed the child by the arm and yanked him to his feet.

'VERSACE! GET UP OF THE FUCKING FLOOR!' she stormed. Order restored, the two women sat down and Versace and friends went to play in the children's corner. The young 'wag' sat, mouth slightly open, with a vacant expression like a fish that had just been caught and clubbed, while her large friend glared round the room.

Andy had never been a snob –far from it – but seeing these two young women made him realise why certain sections of society looked down their nose at working class people – or the 'underclass', as they were now known. He recalled a line from a song – for the life of him he couldn't remember the name of the song or who sang it – that went, 'Who wants to be a man of the people, when there's people like you?'

A nurse appeared with a clipboard and called 'Tess Baker?' Andy and Tess got up and followed the nurse through to one of the scanning rooms.

'OK, Tess, get on the bed and make yourself comfortable. I'll be back in a minute and then we'll do your scan.' The nurse left them alone and Tess got on the bed. 'Are you excited?'

'I am now,' Andy replied.

'Did you see those two girls in reception? My God! How can their treat their children like that?'

'I know. Makes you wonder why they have them at all.'

'For the benefits. Have a few kids you get a house paid for and child allowances so you can afford your booze and fags,' said Tess, smiling.

'Steady on now – jumping to conclusions a bit! They might be fine upstanding citizens with PhDs, earning six figures.'

'Sarcasm is the lowest form of wit, Mr Baker,' Tess admonished him. 'If someone looks, talks and acts a certain way, what are we supposed to think? They're called stereotypes for a reason – they are just that!'

Andy smiled wryly – he certainly couldn't fault her logic. 'Didn't they teach you at uni not to judge a book by its cover?' he teased.

'Books, yes. People – no. And you're a fine one to talk with your ABC demographics, Mr Advertising. Don't you spend all day every day playing on clichés and stereotypes?'

Once again, she was right, and Andy had to grin. Their little debate was interrupted by the return of the nurse. She turned down the lights, prepared the ultrasound scanner and smoothed some gel over Tess's belly. As she began the scan, Andy heard the familiar sound that reminded him of a submarine. He held his wife's hand as, there on the screen, they saw their baby – clear as day. Even though they had been through the process before with Jake, Andy still felt a surge of awe as he witnessed this new life on the screen – a new life that he and Tess had created.

'Do you want to know the sex?' the nurse inquired.

'Yes!' they replied in unison.

'OK, bear with me.' The nurse manoeuvred the wand-like scanner over Tess's belly.

'OK, there we go.' The nurse paused for what felt like an eternity.

'What is it?' said Andy a little impatiently. The nurse smiled.

'It's a girl.'

Tess squeezed Andy's hand and turned her head towards him, tears were welling up. 'We're having a girl. We're going to have a daughter!'

'We are,' Andy nodded. He stared at the screen. A baby girl – a daughter.

And today he would finally meet her – his baby girl – his Maggie. As he boiled the kettle for tea, Andy could hear Tess wailing as the contractions got worse. He poured the tea and took it into the living room – not that it would help anything, but it was what you did under stress. By now Tess was in agony. 'Right, that's it. I'm ringing the hospital again.'

Andy dialled the number for the maternity triage and waited impatiently for an answer. Come on, come on – she's in pain.

'Hello, triage.'

'Hi, it's Andy Baker. I called before about my wife, Tess. She's in labour and having a lot of pain.'

'Have her waters broken yet, Mr Baker?' He presumed the voice belonged to a nurse.

'Not yet.'

'OK. Are her contractions at least two minutes long and thirty seconds apart?'

'They're about a minute and a half, and about every two or three minutes at the moment.'

'Right, if she's in that much pain you can bring her down – but until her waters break we'd just send her home, so it's up to you. I'd give it another few hours and see how she goes.'

'OK, will do. Thank you.' Andy put the phone down, but then saw the expression on Tess's face. 'Come on, we're going.'

As they prepared to go, something occurred to Julie. 'What's happening with Jake?'

'I thought dad was picking him up and taking him back to yours,' said Tess. 'That's what we sorted out.'

'I'll give him a ring. What time does Jake finish school?'

'Quarter past three,' said Andy.

'You two get going. I'll lock up and follow you down,' Julie took charge.

Andy helped Tess into the car and put her bag on the back seat. 'So, here we go.' He started the engine and pulled out of the drive. He threaded his way through the side streets and on to the main road. 'Not long now, babe. You're doing great.'

'Ooooh! Arrrgh!'

'Come on, sweetheart. I love you. You're so brave.'

'Arrrrrrgh!' The contractions were getting worse – longer and more frequent – and Andy put his foot down. As they approached a set of traffic lights he muttered under his breath, 'Don't change. Don't change!'

'Andy, brake! BRAKE!' Tess yelled, as they lurched to a halt. 'You don't have to drive like an idiot, just get us there in one piece.'

The lights changed and they set off again. Andy didn't remember the drive being this long when they had had a dry run a few days before. What seemed like hundreds of roads, roundabouts, junctions and traffic lights later they arrived at the maternity unit car park and drew up close to the doors. Someone somewhere had understood that women in labour really didn't need to walk far.

At reception young nurse was on duty.

'Hi, I rang before. My name's Andy Baker. As you can see, Tess is in a lot of pain.'

'Have her waters broken yet?'

'Not yet – but the pain is getting unbearable,' Tess cut in. 'Arrrrrrrgh, ooh, oooh, ooooooh.' As the contraction subsided, something on the nurse's face suggested that they would be meeting Maggie very soon.

'OK, sweetheart, let's get you examined.' The nurse picked up the phone and they heard her relay what was going on. 'Right, someone will take you though and examine you in just a minute.'

Suddenly there was an audible splash and a puddle appeared at Tess's feet. Almost at the same moment a midwife arrived with a wheel chair. 'Mrs Baker? Oh! I see! Let's get you seen to.'

The nurse helped Tess into the wheel chair and they set off for the ward. The midwife wheeled Tess into a room with four empty beds, showed her to one of them and the nurse closed the curtains around them. 'All right, sweetheart, what's your name?'

'Tess – and this my husband, Andy.'

'OK Tess, let's get you undressed and then we can see what we've got.' The nurse was business-like and reassuring. Andy got out the nightie they had bought just this occasion, and Tess slipped it on and sat back on the bed. The midwife laid a large paper towel over Tess's lower half to protect her dignity and began the examination.

She felt around under the towel as if she was looking in the bottom of a handbag for her keys, but finally she looked up and removed her latex gloves. She smiled at Tess, 'Well, Tess, you're a good seven centimetres dilated.'

'I am?' Tess was more surprised than anyone.

'This baby is well on its way, so it's a good job you came in when you did. We'll get you over to the delivery suite and get you settled,' the midwife explained.

As she left the room, Andy kissed Tess's forehead and held her hand.

'I'm so very proud of you.' He was gently stroking her hair to calm her when the curtain flew back and Julie, flustered and out of breath, lurched in.

'Bloody hell! Thought I'd never get here. Don't worry – I've spoken to your dad. He's going to get Jake from school.' She turned to Andy, 'He also said he's got Jake's present from his little sister with him in the car.'

'Oh, brilliant – I forgot all about that.' He and Tess had decided that Jake might feel left out and resentful with all the attention that would be lavished on Maggie, so they came up with the idea of a present from his new baby sister – a Spiderman costume. Jake was into all the superheroes and they knew he would love it.

The midwife whisked Tess away in a wheelchair with Andy and Julie in hot pursuit. The delivery suite was a large room with a bed, an en-suite bathroom with full-size bath, and a 'birthing couch'. Everything had been designed to be as relaxing and natural as possible – but the banks of medical equipment and monitors were a stark reminder that things could go wrong. Andy found himself looking at the resuscitation equipment and had a momentary vision from his darkest nightmares.

Tess eased herself on to the bed and Andy and Julie took the seats on either side. Another midwife and joined them and the two of them took charge at the business end.

'Come on sweetheart push.'

Tess pushed, and pushed as Andy held her hand and whispered, 'Come on babe, you can do this. You can do it. Push, babe. Push.'

'Come on darling – you're doing great. Not long now,' Julie encouraged her.

Andy turned his head to face the bed – there was only so much he wanted to see. 'Come on babe, push. Push,' he whispered. Tess would tell him later that at that moment she wanted to punch him in the face, and that he was like an annoying fly she wanted to swat away.

'Come on Tess, one more big push,' said the midwife.

Then Andy heard it – he heard his newborn daughter cry for the first time. It was like heaven itself had opened up and sent them this gift. As he turned his head to see this miracle, one of the midwives was bringing her up to meet her parents. She placed her gently on Tess's chest and now, all the pain forgotten, tears of happiness streamed down her face. 'Oh, hello baby girl. Hello Maggie.' Her voice was full of maternal love and compassion.

Andy felt his own eyes pricking as he looked at his daughter. He had had the same feeling when Jake was born – an overwhelming feeling of love. In that moment he knew he would do anything for this child – as he would for Jake. 'Hello, Maggie' he said.

The nurses busied themselves putting Tess back together and Julie left to call her husband to tell him the good news. Andy stayed with Tess and soon, as Tess fell asleep, he found himself alone with his new-born daughter, now settled in a cot. He nudged it gently back and forth and gazed in wonder at the precious little parcel in front of him.

Only a couple of hours old, baby Maggie knew nothing about the world she had entered. She knew nothing about life, love, happiness, sorrow or grief. She didn't yet know the difference between right and wrong – good and evil. She had no idea about money, religion, politics, class or gender. She didn't know anything. Andy and Tess would have to teach her – forge her into a good person – or not, as can sometimes happen. They would have to do all this. They had brought her into this world, and it was their responsibility to look after her. What would she become? What would she look like? What would she sound like? Andy smiled at all this that was to come over the next years. He felt was humbled by the awesome task facing him. 'I won't let you down, Maggie,' he murmured.

Tess was still sleeping, so he quietly slipped out and told the nurse he was going to make a phone call. Would she let Tess know where he was if she woke up?

Outside, it was getting dark. A few smokers hung around the front doors as he got out his phone out and searched his contacts – D for 'DAD'. Andy's parents had emigrated to Spain after his dad retired after thirty years at an aircraft manufacturer, and had received a generous pension. Now the days of jobs for life and well-earned pensions had gone, and Andy and Tess would be lucky to have a state pension by the time they retired.

He waited for the unfamiliar ring tone then his father's voice answered. 'Hola, Senor Baker!' Then before he could get a word in, 'Has she had it? Do I have a granddaughter?'

'She has, and you do. Born about an hour ago. Seven pounds and six ounces, and both mum and baby doing fine.'

'FUCKING MARVELLOUS! CONGRAT-ULATIONS!' his father was roaring down the phone, and Andy held the phone away from his ear.

'Right then, better book some flights. Hold on, let me get your mum.'

From a couple of thousand miles away Andy heard his dad shout his mum, 'ANNE, ANNE, IT'S ANDY! TESS HAS HAD THE BABY!' Andy could hear footsteps as his mother put on a turn of speed quite rare in a woman her age. Then it was her voice on the phone.

'Andy, Andy, can you hear me? So she's arrived!'

'Yes mum, you have a granddaughter!'

Andy could hear a choke in his mother's voice as she went on, 'That's fantastic sweetheart. Congratulations. Your dad and I will be on the next flight over we can get.'

'OK, let me know the details when you get them.'

'And Tess – is she OK? No complications?'

'She's fine mum, both of them are doing fine.'

'Well, give them my best and tell her we'll be having a drink or two over here to wet the baby's head.'

'I will, mum.'

'I love you very much Andrew. I'm so proud of you, my daughter in-law and my TWO grandchildren! I can't wait to see you all.' His mother sounded as if she was about to lose it, and Andy's father took the phone from her. 'Andy, your mum and I just want you to know…' he struggled to get the words out, 'we just want to you know, that we're both very proud of the man you've become, and well, I couldn't ask for a better son,' he said.

It was Andy's turn to wobble, and he felt tears pricking behind his eyes.

'I know dad, I know. Thank you – for everything.'

'All right then, I'll ring you when we've booked our flights and congratulations again. 'Bye son.'

''Bye dad.' He put the phone back in his pocket, wiped his eyes and went back to the hospital. The automatic doors didn't open as he approached, so he took a step back and tried again. Nothing. A man who was having a cigarette told him that the doors were locked the after six for security reasons, and he would have to buzz them to open it.

Andy looked at the silver panel by the side of the door and pressed the call button. 'Hello, security.'

'Hello, er, hi. My wife's just had baby and I need to get back in.'

'OK sir, here you go.'

He was just walking in as the doors opened – then Andy Baker was suddenly back in the present. He was stuck in the lift in the Four Freedoms Tower – trapped in this little box with a lunatic who was pointing a gun at him. His comfortable daydream was over and he was petrified. How was he going to get out of this? He just wanted to go home to his family. He hoped that the authorities might know something about the young man he shared this space with – perhaps they might be waiting for him downstairs – after all, that was their job. Wasn't it?

10

On a quiet cul de sac in one of the nicer suburbs of London, the dawn cast a rusty glow across the dew-covered grass and frosted cars. Inside one of the middle-class semi-detached houses, two sleeping forms in the dark bedroom were suddenly woken by the phone. John Taylor reached out from under the warm duvet and picked it up.

'Hello,' he mumbled, still not fully awake but acutely aware that a call this early would not be good news.

'Inspector, it's Jamie, sir. You need to come in right away. We have some new information.'

Inspector Taylor sat up and rubbed his eyes with his free hand. 'Can't it wait till later?'

The young officer on the other end of the phone paused for a second. 'No, sir. We believe an attack is imminent.'

John Taylor felt as if someone had thrown ice-cold water over him. He reached over and turned on the bedside light. 'Are you sure?'

'You need to come in now, sir.'

'I'm on my way.' He got out of bed and as he pulled clothes from the wardrobe, the form beneath the duvet stirred and the tousled head of his still-sleepy wife emerged. 'You have to go, don't you?'

'Something's come up,' as he got dressed.

'Why did I ever marry a copper?'

'Because the uniform turns you on,' he smiled as he walked over and kissed her forehead.

'You don't wear one any more,' she murmured, as she turned over.

'I won't be long'. He turned off the light and as he made his way downstairs he heard his wife's muffled voice, 'Whatever.'

The car was frozen. There was no time to wait for the screen heaters to do their work, so he went back into the house to fetch the kettle. As he waited for the water to boil, he thought about the morning that lay ahead. Jamie had said they suspected an attack was imminent. Why did he ever take this job? Head of Scotland Yard's counter-terrorist unit. It looked good on paper, but in reality he was nothing more than a scapegoat. Since he'd taken the job six months ago, they had foiled four would-be tragedies, and not a word in the media. But if they failed – if they couldn't stop one – he would be the first to go. That was the price of being in this line of work. He didn't want medals or fame, but it would be nice to get some recognition once in a while, instead of having his hands tied by political bullshit and his budget being cut.

He heard a key in the front door. Great, all he needed now was Mark.

The burley eighteen-year-old strutted into the kitchen. 'What you doing up at this time?' he inquired, as he opened the fridge. 'Pakis up to no good again?' he said laughing.

'Make more noise – the people in the next street didn't hear you.' Ignorant little shit, he thought, willing the kettle to boil.

'So, you and your boys beat anyone up lately?' Mark pressed, as he tucked into the leftovers from dinner.

'There's time yet,' John shot back.

'I don't think mum would approve of that, would she, John?'

John Taylor was a patient man, however, his wife's son tested that patience to the limit. He would love nothing more than to beat the living crap out of the snotty-nosed little sod. But he wasn't his son, so it wasn't his place – at least, that was what his wife said whenever he tried to discipline Mark. The late nights, the backchat, the drugs – they were all part of having children, or so she said.

The kettle finally boiled and John went outside to defrost the car, leaving Mark with his anger and cynicism. John hated the way Mark focused his anger on him – it wasn't his fault his dad went off with another woman. Christ… in those days he was still on the beat.

He took the kettle back into the house, where he found Mark pouring himself a glass of the very expensive whiskey that John had been bought for Christmas. 'What do think you're doing?'

'What does it look like, old man?'

'Just put it down. I think you've had enough,' John said firmly as he took the bottle away.

'You know what, John?' said Mark. 'I hope the Taliban blow you up, mother-fucker,' he spat, as he collapsed on to the couch.

John turned to Mark as he put the bottle away.' Just remember, it's your mother I'm fucking, you little cunt.' With which he strode out of the house and got in the car.

As he pulled out of the drive he immediately regretted getting angry at Mark. For some reason he always managed to rub him up the wrong way. The good thing was that Mark was probably too drunk to remember. He couldn't dwell on that now – right now he had more pressing concerns.

If an attack was being planned for today it meant that the intelligence they had been gathering on a suspected cell was useless.

He put down the window and let the crisp morning air clear his head. John had always had a hard time separating his professional and home lives. On the whole he succeeded – he wouldn't bring his work home and wouldn't let problems with his family affect the way he did his job. However, it was a difficult balancing act and sometimes the stress of his job would erupt at home in bursts of anger, unintentionally directed at the people he loved.

His wife's understanding only went so far – she didn't see the inspector – she just saw John. As an inspector, his job was to protect society from those who would destroy it, but at home John's job was to be a loving husband and father and look after his family. His family. John Taylor had never thought of himself as a family man – he'd never wanted it. Bachelorhood had suited him – he could go where he wanted, when he wanted and with whom he wanted, and could concentrate on his career. All that had changed the day he met Amy.

A few of the lads were going for a drink after a shift and had persuaded John to come along. He'd said he would only stay for one – he had an exam to prepare for. There was the usual bullshit talk about work and football, then, as John went to get a round in, he'd stopped off at the toilets. As he pushed the door it flew back at him and suddenly he was looking at the most beautiful woman he had ever seen. She just smiled at him, said sorry and brushed past him leaving an enticing waft of perfume.

Emboldened by three pints, John turned and stared as she walked back to her friends, transfixed by the skin-tight, curve-hugging leggings and baggy, backless top. For some reason, he decided to stay for a few more rounds and after a chaser towards the end of the evening, he finally went over to her table.

He had given the girls some drink-fuelled blarney about illegal activities going on at their table, and that as a police officer would have to join them.

Through some miracle that he still didn't understand, they'd let him sit down instead of giving him a firm brush-off.

That was ten years ago, now. He and Amy had started seeing each other, and for the first month or so she would not let him come back to her house, and they always ended up at John's flat. By the time she finally told him about her two kids, Mark and Lisa, and how her ex-husband had walked out on them for another woman, it was too late – John was head over heels in love.

Which head he was employing, however, was a matter for debate. Amy was a very attractive woman and more than once his friends told him to stop thinking with his emotional brain – she might be great in bed, they told him, but she's got a lot of baggage, and he had his career to think about. But John didn't care. Sure, the sex was amazing – but there was so much more to it than that as, not just a lover, she became his best friend.

As for the kids, he came to love them as if they were his own, and on Father's Day one year Mark and Lisa (he suspected with some prompting from Amy) bought him a mug, which bore the legend, 'Anyone can father a child, It takes a Man to be a Dad'. That was when John Taylor realised he'd become a family man.

Right now, though, he was a police officer – an inspector. He pushed all thoughts of home from his mind and concentrated on the problem at hand, all the things he needed to do started swirling round his head.

He arrived at the office, parked the car, and grabbed his ID badge that gave him access to the building. Swiping through the magnetically locked doors, he headed for the third floor – the home of the Yard's counter-terrorist division.

The nerve-centre of operations was at the end of a long corridor with glass-walled offices on either side – a large room full of desks covered in electronic monitors, the walls hung with maps and building plans.

The room was buzzing with activity – 'organised chaos' as John saw it, and it seemed ironic that they were there to prevent chaos and maintain order.

'Right, somebody tell me what's going on,' he said. A younger man, Jamie who had called him earlier, hurried over.

'Sir, GCHQ intercepted an email from one of the cells we have been tracking to an unknown man named Khalid.'

'And?' John took a moment to gather his thoughts. For once the Government Communications Headquarters – the agency responsible for all electronic and signals intelligence, and the people who the public considered as invaders of privacy – had done their job.' What do we know about this Khalid?'

Jamie sat down at one of the monitors and in a few key strokes a picture of Khalid outside a mosque appeared on the screen. 'His real name is Josef Reiniger. He came over on a student visa eighteen months ago and is a regular at the mosque we have had under surveillance. He's a German national, we don't know if he was already converted to Islam when he came over, or has been converted since arriving, but from the information we've been getting from Interpol, I'd say he was sent here specifically for this. We've asked GCHQ for electronic signals interception, including online.'

John Taylor stared at the picture on the screen and began to assess the situation. 'Fucking hell,' he mused. The game had changed. For months, rumours amongst European law enforcement agencies had been circulating about white Europeans converting to Islam – the kind of Islam that preached hatred towards the infidel, the kind taught by Al Qaida. At first John had dismissed it. Why would a person raised in a predominately Christian and even more secular society want to become a Muslim? Fair enough, that was freedom – personal choice – but to become an extremist just didn't make any sense.

When the 'war on terror' began it was a natural, albeit racist assumption that all members of Al Qaida were dark skinned. After all, over ninety per cent of the Islamic world was of either Middle Eastern, Asian or African descent. The other major problem facing the authorities was that many western countries, especially Britain, had a large indigenous Muslim population.

During the course of his work, John Taylor had studied the Qur'an and, like The Bible, it preached tolerance and charity, but like any religious text – or any text for that matter – it had been misinterpreted and twisted to suit the aims of a few.

So now absolutely anybody was a potential threat. For some reason an image of Mark flashed through his mind – but guilt could wait.

'Do we know his location?'

Jamie looked him in the eye, a shadow of fear spread across his face. 'They managed to track his location from the internet signal from his laptop, and we think…'

'Just tell me where he is.'

'Four Freedoms Tower, sir.'

'Jesus fucking Christ. The tallest building in the city! You can see the thing for miles. Is that the target?' Not waiting for an answer, John Taylor grabbed the nearest phone. A plan was beginning to form in his head and he was going to make damn sure no one died today.

'That building has a twenty-four-hour concierge service…' And then, to the phone, 'Yes, hello. Can you put me through to the Four Freedoms building?' As he waited to be connected he felt got that familiar churning in the pit of his stomach – a mixture of adrenaline, nervousness and fear.

'Good morning, Four Freedoms Tower, Bob speaking. How can I help you?'

'Hello, I'm Inspector Taylor, Met Police. I need some urgent information.'

'OK sir, what do you need to know?'

'Has there been any unusual activity tonight or in the past few days?'

'No sir, it's been quiet as a tomb. One of the lifts is stuck at the moment, but that's nothing new.'

Taylor thought for a moment. 'You're sure, no one has tried to gain access, or has been acting strangely outside?'

'No sir, we are pretty tight on security here.'

Taylor gazed down at the desk as if trying to find an answer to a puzzle. 'Do you have records and a list of residents?'

'Of course we do, sir.'

'OK, I'm looking for a young German student. His name is Josef Reiniger but he may go by the name Khalid. Does he sound familiar? Does he live in the building?'

'I'm sorry sir, but even if I did know this gentleman, I couldn't give out any information due to data protection.' Bob maintained stolidly.

'For God's sake man, this is no time for 'data protection' – I'm a police officer conducting an investigation. People's lives may be at risk. Do you know him?'

'Sir. All due respect, but you are a voice on the end of a phone. You could be anyone, and I could get into serous trouble for disclosing personal information about residents. Some of them are very protective of their privacy.'

Seething with frustration, Taylor could scarcely believe what he was hearing. This was ridiculous. 'Fine. Thanks for your help.' He slammed the phone down and turned to Jamie. 'Come on, we're going down there. Grab a couple of uniforms and meet me outside.'

Despite all his years of experience, Inspector John Taylor couldn't even begin to imagine what the situation would be when he got to the Four Freedoms Tower.

'Sir, there's a report for you from GCHQ, compiled from various sources detailing the cell's operations over the last view years.' Jamie offered.

'Thanks, bring it with you. I'll read it in the car.' Thank God for the whiz kids over at GCHQ, John thought to himself. They must've hacked into his computer and gone though his email account. That was how they operated – one email address that every member had access to. The clever thing was no emails were ever sent, making it impossible to trace – unless you happened to know who the suspect was – then it was simple matter of hacking into their computer and retrieving the information. The hardest part was getting permission – unlike them, the authorities still had to follow the law and provide just cause and evidence that their was a credible threat before they were allowed to hack into a private citizen's computer or bug their phones.

He didn't have time for the politics or red tape right now. Right now he just had to make sure no body was blown to bits today.

In the car, Jamie handed John the report. 'Here you go sir, hot off the press.' The inspector opened the file and began to read.

Background

Information pertaining to the background of the recruiters of Josef Reiniger to the terror network is complex but as evidence has shown, those involved must be classified as being highly dangerous.

The main perpetrators were recruited in the early 1980s, when they were trained in combat over in Afghanistan. It is known they took active part in the smuggling of weapons to anti-Soviet forces, as well as raising funds for their cause at home as well as in several European countries, but have focussed most of their efforts in Germany and the UK.

In Germany, they centred most of their activities around the East of Berlin and Hamburg, where they purchased small office space at the end of the Cold War and converted the premises into a low-key and inconspicuous mosque.

According to intelligence sources from the German police, the leader of the mosque was a Saudi national who travelled freely between Saudi Arabia, Yemen, Afghanistan and Pakistan, where he would also 'introduce' new recruits to the training camps on the borders of Pakistan and Afghanistan.

New recruits were also used to obtain further funding from inside Saudi Arabia and, as the activity of the Imam increased, so did funding for the East German Mosque. For example, an unknown Saudi source is said to have paid the equivalent of over £300,000 for 6,000 copies of a thirty-page booklet.

Recruits were also used to promote the mosque and various causes inside Palestine and Iraq where, after the Iraqi invasion of Kuwait, money and support were offered to fight against Saddam Hussein, with the hope of obtaining post-war support from inside Kuwait.

It is known that the mosque ran into some public conflicts with far-right elements within Germany, who were sympathetic to the Iraqi government and who, before the liberation of Kuwait, had actually visited leading Iraqi officials with a view to providing military support to the Iraqi regime in the event of an attack.

Intelligence sources from inside Iraq reported how far-right groups were offered both sanctuary around Baghdad and positions within the Iraqi military, in exchange for far-right support against military intervention.

At the end of the Gulf War, it is known that the mosque paid a lot of attention to the conflict within the Palestine authority, where they publicly supported suicide bombing as a 'legitimate line of defence against Zionist aggression', while claiming that European support for Israel was a cause of the high levels of poverty and unemployment in the Eastern Germany after reunification.

The mosque sought to capitalise on the instability around the former Soviet Union and the Middle East, targeting in particular young refugees and asylum-seekers, offering them jobs in local takeaway food outlets, print shops and money transfer bureaux.

The mosque had also established a 'family service', which offered support in housing and provided Islamic education for children. According to a child services report, most of the housing was cheap but totally condemned as wires were found hanging loose, gas supplies were not checked, broken windows remained unrepaired and many of the rooms were found with loose plaster on the walls, and the furniture was below minimum standard.

Children were found sleeping on damp mattresses on the floor; their ability to communicate outside their native language was rudimentary if not non-existent. One young man who had escaped, reported to the authorities that to cover the 'rent' he was forced to prostitute himself to male clients introduced by the landlord.

Surveillance of the two food outlets showed that, while outwardly used as regular businesses, repeated irregularities have occasioned alarm, leading to inspections by the tax and local authorities, and raids relating to human trafficking, tax evasion, general health and safety, and concern relating to comments to local residents about 'the German way of life' and Holocaust denialism.

The ownership of the food outlets has changed repeatedly, following actions by the authorities but the commonality in ownership is that each new manager is a regular attendee of the mosque, except in one case where an arrest was made and conviction obtained because according to the name provided, the new manager had been dead for five years.

One of the members of the mosque, who moved to the United Kingdom in 1986, is now residing in a maximum security prison serving four life sentences, having been found guilty of inciting and recruiting jihadists to fight Allied forces in Afghanistan.

According to intelligence sources in the United Kingdom, this person made contact through a Saudi national who ran a market stall in the North of England, selling children's clothes to raise money for their cause.

Based in the North West of England, this market stall drew little attention from the British authorities because of its ability to blend into the local population by employing local converts to Islam.

Concern about this person's behaviour and activities was only aroused after an illegal street stall had been set up from which he was found handing out literature denouncing the state of Israel, employing terminology encouraging people to carry out independent acts of vandalism against British military venues.

He was first approached on the street stall by local police officers, when he denied any intent to cause harm. He was put under continued surveillance by under-cover anti-terror officers and was found to be stalking the activities of a local military charity.

Following his arrest, other suspects were interviewed, including a series of British converts who each denied any involvement, and denied witnessing or being party to any discussions relating to his activities in recruiting or distributing terror-based material.

According to one of the interviewees, who had known this person since his entry to the United Kingdom in the 1980s, discussions at the clothing stall caused concern among the family of one worker, who objected strongly to his son's employment because, as this witness claimed, 'there was a man who used to come along, whose views on Islam were quite strong and opinionated, but few who worked there would take him seriously, as everybody in charge (of the market stall) seemed quite nice.'

Further investigation allowed us to trace the family of this person to a former mining area of Newcastle, where we interviewed both parents at length about their son. It transpired that they hadn't seen him for over a decade and it later emerged that he was now dead, having been killed in air raid in Kabul.

The parents recalled how their son had started working on the clothing stall in early 1987 to earn some extra money while he was studying religion and politics at a local college. Prior to this employment, he had a substantial circle of friends, was involved in sports and other recreational activities, had a busy social life and had always had an awareness of global events.

Within six months of starting work on the clothing stall, he converted to Islam and gradually distanced himself from his family, on the grounds that they did not understand or support his new-found faith, and believed them to be racially hostile to those involved with his religion. He went so far as to accuse his parents of denying him his rightful religion at birth.

In the interview, both parents and even a sibling described how they tried to accommodate his new religion, but he insisted that he could not attend the family home at Christian festivals, participate in birthday celebrations or even be present at the family home when there were female non-relatives present, as these were the conditions set down by his faith.

His sister described him as having been 'taken over', no longer able to 'hold an opinion of his own but seemed to be reading from a script. He would often quote passages from the Qur'an relating to how I dressed, who I went out with, the food I ate and my choice of career'. He also objected to women being in employment,

'As in Islam, the man is to provide for the needs of the family as instructed by God'.

Details surrounding the man's death in Kabul are sketchy, with two different accounts being given by local residents and the person with whom he had gone to Afghanistan. When interviewed by the military, local residents reported him as regularly carrying weapons and travelling around with suspected Taliban fighters, while his companion claimed he was there to assist with humanitarian aid for those adversely affected by the US/UK military presence.

Others who worked on the stall, while denying any involvement, have regularly attended anti-war activities across the United Kingdom, and one has a photograph of himself posted on a social networking site, proudly holding a banner calling for the destruction of the state of Israel.

Another person, currently under surveillance by British authorities, is known to have helped to supply arms to insurgents in Iraq, travelling frequently between 2000 and 2006 to the Kingdom of Jordan, where he is suspected of having met up with Abu Rishda.

It is known from American sources, that until the end of the SOFA agreement, which saw the full withdrawal of US troops from Iraq on New Year's Eve 2011, that this person would often fly from London to Cairo, where he has twice been reported in the Gaza Strip but has also been found to be using the Egyptian capital to make a connection via the port of Aqaba into Jordan or accessing transport to gain entrance into Northern Iraq.

In an effort to raise funds for their organisation, it is known that several front organisations have been established in the United Kingdom and they are using charitable status to avoid tax and to provide a spurious legitimacy for their activities.

It is known that money is regularly transferred between these front organisations through the online services such as Paypal. One of these groups is a Dawa group to support the 'physical and emotional well-being of the Islamic community'. This charity, whose financial details were obtained from the Charities Commission, was found to have only made £7,890 in a year but intelligence has found the number to exceed that amount by over £10,000.

Investigations have also discovered that further money has changed hands as a direct result of human trafficking, where fleeing refugees have been forced to hand over up to £20,000 for transport from their country of origin and safe passage into and relocation in mainland Europe. Some of these networks have been successfully closed down by border controls, but there is concern, and there is currently investigation under way into these networks gaining access through identity theft.

Another issue currently under investigation is the network's infiltration into several anti-war organisations in the UK and Europe, where members are known to be active. Invitations have been issued to prominent preachers who have been known to promote terrorism and militia activities against Allied countries.

The number of visa requests to relevant authorities has increased, with many requests for entry for known imams from various Middle Eastern and north African countries. When refusals were issued, protests by applicant organisations have immediately followed in response.

Requests for visas have been requested for known paramilitary groups who have carried out acts of ethnic cleansing against religious minorities, and who have actively participated in the murder of US and UK forces, under the aegis of attending peace conferences.

It is worth noting, that there is a consistent pattern in the appeals and protests in response to visa refusal. These usually involve the same people, and any media coverage is normally provided by agencies hostile to British interests. Increasing agitation activity by protesters has been observed on social networking sites such as Facebook and Twitter.

We are increasingly concerned at the number of false profiles being established by these people, who often set up a variety of accounts using different names and contact details, but where the information they provide is often similar or the same and quite often uses sources which are factually inaccurate or misleading.

These multiple accounts are regularly used to publicly harass or intimidate people, and also to give the public impression of being more numerous than they are, and of having greater public support than they do.

Investigations into one suspect revealed that, contrary to his claim of being a twenty-year-old anti-war law graduate, he was 47 years old and unemployed, with a previous conviction for grievous bodily harm.

In another case, a British woman whose family background was in the Irish Republican movement promoted an on-line identity claiming to be a Libyan whose family had been killed in a NATO bomb attack.

One man was arrested for openly giving out information on line about the movements of a team of genuine peace activists in Iraq, and the movement and locations of prominent Iraqi politicians, which resulted in the peace activists being kidnapped and one person being killed. The activists were eventually only released as a direct result of British Special Forces responding to full intelligence reports on the kidnappings.

John Taylor closed the file and gave it back to Jamie. 'Well, that makes interesting reading. So basically we know fuck all about the actual guy we're after – this Josef Reiniger.'

'Seems that way, sir.'

Reading the report brought it home to John how monumental the task of fighting these people was, and how far-reaching it was. But how can you fight something you can't see?

'Wonderful,' John murmured under his breath.

11

A deafening silence filled the lift. Khalid stared at the ceiling. Andy looked down at his shoes. There was no sound for what seemed like an eternity. Andy wondered what the young man opposite him had been through to make him this way. He had read in the papers about a growing number of western Europeans converting to Islam. Was he himself bigoted? All he knew about Islam was what he had read and heard in the media and what his friends at work told him. Was that wrong? Should he be more aware? But after all, the UK was a predominantly Christian country… wasn't it? When the monarch is crowned they are proclaimed 'Defender of the Faith', not 'faiths'. The law of the land is ultimately derived from the teachings of The Bible, not the Qur'an or the Torah.

In the Middle Ages, thousands of young English soldiers went to the Holy Land on the crusades. Now, in the 21st Century, Andy could not help but think of the wars in Iraq and Afghanistan – and then of all the progress made down the centuries in science, technology. In spite of this, mankind still fought over religion. The politicians would disagree; they would say it's about something else – freedom, and an end to tyranny and oppression.

The conspiracy theorists would say it was about oil and minerals, and the imperialist west exploiting poor countries for the profit of its corporations.

All this could be true, but right now to Andy Baker, it was about nothing more than religion – about ideology and two opposing forces vying for dominance in the same environment.

It didn't matter what colour this young man's skin was, what language he spoke or what nationality passport he held. Andy knew that Khalid believed what he was saying to be true. He had his strong faith and implicit trust in his own ideological dogma – and that made him a truly terrifying force to be reckoned with.

'Where are you from?' Andy ventured.

Khalid slowly turned his gaze on Andy. 'It does not matter where I'm from, but where I am going that is important.'

'I don't understand. Why have you come here to kill yourself and loads of other people? You said we are your enemy. Why are we? How?' Andy was genuinely mystified. Khalid's face filled with surprise.

'You don't know? You really are an ignorant pig aren't you, Andy? Your whole culture, your whole ideology is disgusting to us. You have no honour. You treat your women as equals and let them dress like whores. You allow your leaders to abuse and invade other nations with no just cause. All you care about is making a profit – and you will do anything, even kill, for your precious money. You let homosexuals marry each other and spit in the face of the Almighty. Your entire way of life is an insult to Allah, and you must be punished in his name.'

Andy grimaced at this religious zealot's words. 'So you want to kill us all because we offend you? What about tolerance? You speak about the way we live. It's called freedom – freedom to choose for yourself the way you live your life. Freedom to worship any God you like, love anyone you want to, dress any way you want – and you can do all this in safety and comfort. If that offends you, get over it. Who the hell are you – or anyone else who would get what they want by killing – to tell me my way of life offends their god?'

Khalid brought the gun up and pointed it straight at Andy, who for a brief moment thought this was the end; the anger in Khalid's soul filled the lift. 'What gives you people the right to force your way of life on others? You speak of tolerance – what makes you think the rest of the world wants democracy and Google and Starbucks, and all your western decadence? The truth is, your so-called freedom is just a smokescreen so you can get at the resources of the Islamic world. You want to turn every nation into a puppet state of the west. I realised not long after I moved here that no amount of tolerance can change how different we are. This is a war, Andy, and in every war there has to be a winner.' Khalid lowered the gun, giving Andy a tiny spark of hope that he might still get out of this, and maybe even get through to Khalid.

'You're talking about war. Killing unarmed strangers isn't war, it's murder. I'm not a soldier – I'm a Joe nobody. I haven't done a thing wrong to you and you think I'm your enemy because of where I was born. Look, there are lots of problems in the world – that's not my fault. I just want to live my life in peace. You know what? I don't even vote. I think they're all a lying pack of scumbags, out to line their own pockets, so I just think there's no point. A lot of people I know are the same. People are more interested in the football and reality TV than they are in politics and world affairs. Most people in this country really don't care about you or your god or your views.

But when you commit these crimes, we sit up and take notice. Because what we do care about are our families and friends, and if they get hurt or killed, then we all become soldiers, and we take a stand. Do you really think that you're the first people ever to want to force their views on us? Others have tried and they have all failed. This country's got plenty of problems – that's the price of freedom – but if you want to take that away, watch out. Go on, shoot me. Then when the lift opens you will be arrested and you won't be going to your god.'

Without a word, Khalid raised the gun and aimed it at Andy's eyes.

He pulled back the hammer, which made a loud, sickening click.

12

'Your dead Andy, hand it over,' said Rick.

Andy wasn't in the lift, or in Four Freedoms Tower. He didn't have a gun in his face and he wasn't in fear of his life. He wasn't even in London –he was back at the flat he lived in at university over a decade ago. He shared the flat with Rick, his best friend whom he'd met on his first day. Rick was one of those people everybody knew – good-looking, confident and a natural at anything he turned his hand to. Most people had a friend like Rick – loved and loathed in equal measure, and Rick was now pestering Andy to give him the remote of the Nintendo 64 they were playing on. 'Come on, Andy, you're dead, mate.'

'One more go,' Andy wheedled.

'No way, mate. Face it, you'd be a shit James Bond.'

Andy reluctantly handed over the remote.

'Thank you,' said Rick, 'now see how a professional does it.' Rick started the game and quickly got further along than Andy had.

'What time's the seminar?' Rick asked, without taking his eyes off the game.

'Two 'til three in the basement with Steve.'

'Lovely – an hour with Comrade Steve. I really need that today,' Rick grumbled.

'He's not that bad.'

'He's a communist fuck!'

Andy laughed at his friend's candid assessment of their lecturer. They were both doing a degree in business and marketing, part of which was a module on Marxism.

Rick completed the level on the game and threw the remote on the coffee table. 'And that, my friend, is how we do that. Maybe I should apply for MI6.'

'I don't think you have the temperament, mate,' Andy goaded.

'I would be an **ace** secret agent,' he said, leaning back on the sofa and lighting a cigarette. 'So, who do you think will be the next Bond?'

'Don't know – Brosnan's pretty good, it'll be hard to find another actor to fill his shoes. He's by far the best since Connery,' Andy offered.

'For shurre,' said Rick in his bad Connery impersonation.

'Hugh Jackman might make a good Bond,' Andy suggested.

'Wolverine? No way, plus he's an Aussie and we know how that turns out. They need to find an unknown Brit to play him.'

'As long as it's not an American,' Andy insisted.

'Too right. I don't think it'd happen though – there'd be uproar. It'd be a like a Brit playing Batman or Superman.' Rick stubbed out his cigarette in the ashtray. 'Come on then, let's get it over with. Then we can get ready for tonight's festivities.'

They collected their things for the upcoming seminar. Andy, ready first as usual, began to tidy the flat, moving some of the many pots into the kitchen and gathering the rubbish from the living room – empty pizza boxes, beer and pop cans, crisp packets and chocolate wrappers.

'Leave them. We'll do it later.' Rick was in the doorway, waiting to go.

'OK, but you can help as well. Don't be sneaking off!'

'I will, I will. I fully intend to get some girls back tonight and it does no good if the place is a shit tip.'

They left the flat, which was actually a room in an old Victorian town house that had been converted into student flats, and set off for the campus.

'So, what time's the gig tonight?' Andy asked.

'We go on at nine. Should be good – just make sure you're not late.' Rick was the lead singer in a rock band, and was very, very good. He had a natural stage presence and was an amazing frontman. Andy was convinced that one day he would be playing sell-out stadium gigs and world tours. The only reason he was at uni was to keep his dad happy. Rick's dad, whom Andy had met only once, didn't think that rock and roll was a good career choice.

'I still can't believe you're playing at Diamonds.'

'I know. It's gonna be ace! Even though it will be full of left-wingers – though to be fair, they're the easiest to play for – as long as you play the right songs.'

Andy smiled. Diamonds was a very popular student venue and had over 3000 capacity, so it was a big night for Rick and the band. It was the night-spot of choice for the university's Labour Party youth wing as well as the more die-hard socialists – the guys who idolised Che Guevara and the CND crowd.

'What you gonna play?' Andy asked.

'Don't know yet. Might give 'em *Run to the Hills* by Iron Maiden – that'll get 'em going. Our

Mike said that's what they listened to in Kuwait before they went in.'

'Have you heard from him lately?'

'I got a letter from him a few weeks ago. He's OK. He's an illiterate bastard anyway, so it takes him about a day to write a letter,' Rick said, smiling. His brother, Mike, was in the army and currently serving in Iraq. He was part of the recent invasion and was due home soon. As much as he tried to hide it, for the past few months Rick had been on tenterhooks. Every time the phone rang in the flat there would be moment of tension – a flash of panic in his eyes. Was it his dad bringing bad news? It got to the point where Andy answered every call.

'When does he get back?'

'End of August we think. It'll be good – you'll have to come down and we'll go on the piss. You and Mike would get on.'

They were nearing the building where the seminar was due to take place. 'Really can't be arsed with this,' Rick sighed.

'An hour – that's all.' They went into the building and headed to the basement where a few rooms were used for small seminars. A gaggle of their fellow students was waiting outside the seminar room. A couple of minutes later, the door opened and their lecturer, Steve, invited them in. Settling in their seats, they took out their pens, notebooks – and a textbook on the writings of Karl Marx.

Steve took his seat at his desk. Late twenties or early thirties, Steve was a walking caricature of a university lecturer – tweed jacket with suede arm patches and glasses. He nudged his glasses up the bridge of his nose with his forefinger. 'So, lets begin where we left off last week. If I'm not mistaken we were having a debate on why a CEOs should earn seven figures when one of his workers earns minimum wage. Does anyone want to start us off?' His eye wandered to Rick. 'Richard, how about you? You were very vocal about this last week. Have you any further thoughts?'

'Yeah. That's life,' Rick announced, to a few muffled laughs.

'Go on please – elaborate.'

Here we go, thought Andy, more locking of horns and butting of heads.

'Well, for me, it's all about individual choices. The CEO, at some point, made a choice to go into business – more than likely holds a degree and higher, and has had to work his way up the ladder, which takes effort and drive. He didn't leave school and get a job as the CEO of a large multinational did he? No. It was down to his own personal choices – and he gets the rewards. Nothing wrong with that.'

'So what about the person who earns minimum wage, say, cleaning the CEO's office – or a low-level worker at the company? Did they make the choice to do that?'

'Well, yeah. They went to school and got the same level of education as the CEO,' Rick persisted.

'Did they?' Steve had the bit between his teeth.

'Yeah.'

'OK, let me put this to you. Do you think class has anything to do with it? The social and economic situation that people are born into? Do you think that has any bearing on what people end up doing in life?' Steve pressed, as Rick grimaced, trying to hide his frustration.

'Like I said, it's down to individual choice. We live in a society where anyone can do or be anything they want to be – it's called freedom.'

'I don't agree.' Steve was throwing down the gauntlet, and Rick being Rick, picked it up.

'OK, let's take the people in this room. As far as I know, none of us are exactly upper class – we're all working or lower-middle class, and we are all here because we want to do well in life. I bet there are loads of people we know of our age – people we went to school with – who right now are working, some of them probably earning minimum wage or on apprenticeships or whatever. Some of them are on the dole – so in twenty years, who's to say that one us won't be a CEO or a successful businessperson, and that the same guys we went to school with – who got exactly the same education we did – won't be working for us or have a minimum wage job? And is that our problem – or theirs?'

Steve gave him a forced smile – half awe-struck, half shocked.

'That's page one of how to be a Tory! "I'm alright Jack – the rest of you can rot".'

'That's not what I said.' Rick was on fire.

'That's exactly what you're saying – and you're right – we do have freedom in this country and having a degree does help in a big way – but it's not as clear-cut as you make out.' Steve paused, waiting for a response that didn't come. 'So, in your opinion, if a person isn't academically minded and doesn't do well at school, they should just accept it? Or should we have a system where everyone, regardless of where their strengths lie, gets the same opportunities?'

Andy rubbed his eyes; this was going to be a very long hour indeed. The age-old argument – the same debate that had been raging for a couple of hundred years about the best way to govern a civilised society which, at it's heart, was all about what type of economic system ruled – free market capitalism, a mixed market economy, or socialism and the nationalisation of some or all of the means of production. It was nothing new. Neither Rick nor Steve was going to come up with an answer – a solution to this problem – all that was going to happen was that an hour's worth of heated discussion would end with Andy getting an earful on the walk back to the flat. Right now Andy didn't care – he just wanted to go back to the flat, chill out for a bit and then get ready for the gig that evening. One of the positive aspects of being Rick's friend was that when he played a gig there were always opportunities to talk to girls. His mind wandered around all the possibilities of the night ahead. He didn't hear the continuing debate; he didn't hear other students piping up with their own thoughts on the subject. The next thing he heard was Steve: 'Right, it looks like we're out of time. Remember to read the passages I've earmarked for next week, and have a good weekend.'

The chairs and desks scraped over the floor as the class rose and left.

Andy wove his way through the crowd to catch up with Rick, who had shot off in a huff – a common outcome of these seminars.

'Wait up, mate,' said Andy, brushing past some students to catch up with Rick. 'Don't let it bother you mate, it's his job to get us to think.'

'He's an obnoxious little prick. With his fucking NHS specs he thinks are fashionable, and that tweed jacket and loafers. He wouldn't dare say half that shit in a bar.' Rick was seething.

'I don't know why you take it so personally, mate. So what? He disagrees with you. Live with it.' For a few brief seconds there was silence, and Andy accorded himself the luxury of thinking the conversation was over and they could turn their attention to something else. But he was wrong.

'There's nothing fucking worse than a Campari socialist,' Rick fumed. Andy rolled his eyes. 'Banging on about the plight of the working class and unions and solidarity. Bet he's worked **lots** of minimum wage jobs, him! A fucking lecturer at university? Dead working class that! I'm sure Orwell met lots of lecturers on the road to Wigan fucking Pier!' Rick was scarcely pausing for breath.

'Have you finished?' Andy inquired.

'I should just knock him out and have done with it! Explode his nose all over his smug fucking face!'

'Yes. Because that's always the best way to win an argument, isn't it? Someone disagrees with you, hit them until they do?'

'Piss off.'

'Oooh Rick, you know what? Now you've hit me and broken my nose, I actually think the way you do! Thank you for making me see the truth! It was your punch that actually woke me up to a lifetime of thinking all wrong. You have changed my opinion with your fist!' Andy delivered his coup de grace in a faux middle-class accent.

The ridicule snapped Rick out of his mood, and he laughed. 'Well, if your gonna take the piss, you can forget about managing the band once we're signed!'

'You! I'd rather manage Guns and Roses – they might be easier to handle.'

As they rounded the corner into their street, Rick's phone rang – he had a text message. He read it and stopped. 'Sorry mate, I have to go, we've got to do a sound check before the gig.'

'That's convenient.'

'What? I have to go. Come on, we'll tidy up later. I'll help you. No, I tell you what, you tidy the flat and I'll get you a bird tonight – you can have one my cast-offs,' he proffered, grinning broadly.

'I tell you what, I'll tidy the flat – again – just do me one favour?'

'What?'

'Stay off the snow!'

Rick, without saying a word started sniffing the air; he put his face up close to Andy's head and began to sniff. He took a step back and stared at Andy wide-eyed. 'Mum? Mum? Is that you?' Rick smiled, turned and walked off to his sound check. Andy called after him, 'You're not a rock star yet, you know!' Rick turned, spread his arms wide and gave him a big cheesy grin. 'No, but I will be one day – so why not live like one now?' He turned and walked on.

Andy heaved a deep sigh as he watched Rick round the corner, then walked back to the flat. He went to his room, dropped his bag on the bed then started to tidy up. A few bin bags, some Mr Muscle and a hoover round, followed by a very liberal dose of lavender air freshener and half an hour later the flat was respectable again. Andy looked round the front room and nodded to himself. He checked the time – a few hours yet, so too early to get ready. He made a cup of tea and went to his bedroom, stretched out on the bed and began to read. It was Voltaire's Philosophical Dictionary, which had been recommended by one of his lecturers. Voltaire may have been a philosopher and writer in the 19th Century, but a lot of what he said all those years ago still made sense today. For all the advances in science and technology, some things never changed – even our basic notion of right and wrong. In Voltaire's time women were considered second-class citizens and the practice of slavery was legal and accepted, yet they hanged murderers and jailed thieves. Andy pondered about who decides what is right and what is wrong? Where does that come from? From people? Are the basics built into to us or do they come from somewhere else?

All these thoughts swirled round Andy's mind as he read and read and read. He closed his eyes for a brief moment. When he opened his eyes, that brief moment had turned into two hours. He checked the time – shit, he was late.

Andy jumped off the bed, put the light on and began to get ready. The flat was in semi-darkness from the dusk outside, the streetlights were not yet on. He flicked the lights on in the living room then went to the bathroom to put the shower on, undressed and grabbed a towel. As he washed his face at the basin he wondered if he should shave – or go with the five-o'clock shadow.

Fuck it, the shadow it would be. He showered quickly, wrapped the towel round his waist and returned to his room. Andy flung the towel on the bed and searched his wardrobe. Which T-shirt to wear? The Stones? Sabbath? Batman? The Stones –everyone likes the stones. He dressed and cheeked himself out in the mirror.

A splash of aftershave and he was ready. Time to go.

He checked the flat one last time, just in case people did end up coming back later, grabbed his jacket then rushed out to the gig venue. In all the haste of getting ready he hadn't checked his phone – four missed calls and two texts, all from Rick. The second one, unflattering though it was, made him smile. 'You better get your fucking ass down here now! We're about to go on, dick-head. The only excuse I will accept for not being here is if someone's sat on your cock! And HE better be worth it – ha ha ha.'

Andy put his phone away as he approached Diamonds. He could hear the music from outside – Rick and his band had already started. As he walked through the doors he was greeted with a burst warm air laden with cigarette smoke and alcohol. Rick was doing his thing on the stage at the other end of the venue – they were well into a cover of *Back in Black* by AC/DC and the crowd were loving it.

Andy battled his way through to the bar, which was reasonably quiet as most people were watching the band. He ordered a bottle of his favourite Labatt's Ice, and watched the show. The place was packed to the rafters – no surprise as Rick's band were actually fantastic and the word had spread quickly.

Out of the corner of his eye, Andy caught a glimpse of a group of girls at the other end of the bar, ordering drinks – chatting and giggling, the way girls in groups do. He tactically manoeuvred himself around to face the bar, pretending he was waiting to be served so he could get a better view. He took a swig of his beer – in his head he was like James Dean or Steve McQueen or Bond. Really cool. He noticed one girl in particular. Fuck me, she's stunning, he thought. He took another swig from his bottle, and took another look. Another sip and another look. This time he made eye contact with her, and unbelievably she smiled at him. What did that mean? Did she want him to go over? Was she interested? Bloody hell, she's beautiful! Andy looked away. Go over. Introduce yourself. What have you got to lose?

'THANK YOU! WE'RE FOUR ZERO! WE'RE GONNA TAKE A SHORT BREAK NOW, BUT WE'LL BE BACK ON SOON, THANK YOU, YOU'RE GREAT!' Rick called from the stage. Andy barely noticed the massive roar of applause or the DJ putting on some background music. He vaguely recognised the song, but paid no attention. Go over you wimp. Introduce yourself. She smiled at you. He took a large gulp form his bottle finishing it off. Courage, man. He prepared himself and as he turned and looked she was gone. Shit. That's what you get with indecision.

He ordered another drink and was staring at the optics behind the bar when he sensed someone arrive next to him at the bar. The barman gave him his drink and Andy paid for it before taking a swig. The barman turned to the person next to Andy. 'What can I get you, luv?'

'Can we have the same again, please? A pitcher of margarita,' she said.

'Coming right up,' said the barman.

Andy turned his head slightly to take a look. It was her. Say something, you muppet – do something.

'Are you a man of wealth and taste then?' she asked. It took Andy a few seconds to realise she was talking to him, then he turned to face her. God, she was beautiful.

'Excuse me?' he asked, smiling. He was not sure what was going on.

'The song,' she said and nodded over to the DJ. Confused, Andy wasn't sure what to say. 'Your T-shirt!' she said, looking hard at it with huge eyes like big beautiful jewels.

'You're a stones fan,' she said, and the penny dropped as Andy heard what song was playing.

'I like to think so,' he said, 'Although I have absolutely no sympathy for Lucifer – he brought it all on himself.' The girl laughed and Andy, impressed with his newfound suavity, carried on, 'I'm Andy,' he said, holding out his hand. They shook hands. 'Tess' she said.

'Nice to meet you, Tess.'

'You too.'

There was an awkward silence as Andy figured out what to say next, 'So do you go here?' he said.

'I do.'

'What you doing?'

'English and journalism,' she replied. 'What about you?'

'Business and marketing.' Whatever confidence Andy had summoned up before was now gone – all that was left was an awkward nervousness, and she knew it too. The barman came back with her order. 'Here you go luv.' He handed her the jug of cocktail, she paid for it and turned to Andy, 'Well, it was nice meeting you, Andy the Stones fan. See you around.'

'It was nice meeting you too, Tess.' Shit shit shit shit, Andy you idiot, do something. She smiled at him and turned to walk away. 'Can I buy you a drink?' he said. Normally this would have been the acceptable thing to do in this situation – you see a girl you like and she likes you enough not to run away, so you ask to buy her a drink. She turned to look at him and raised her eyebrows. 'Think I'm good, thanks,' she said, raising the full cocktail jug slightly.

Andy smiled back at her, defeated. 'Yeah…' He took a swig of his beer and started playing with the label, peeling it off and spinning the bottle in his hand.

'I wouldn't mind one of those, though,' said Tess. 'Let me give to this to my friends and I'll be back in a minute'

'OK, sure,' said Andy, trying his best to look cool when what he wanted to do was jump up and down and fist pump the air. He ordered another bottle of beer for her and in no time she was back next to him.

'That for me?'

'It is.' He was still finding it hard not to be intimidated by her beauty.

'So, Andy, what are you doing here all on your own?'

'I've been waiting for a girl like you,' he said, hoping this sounded suave and not cheesy.

'A girl like me?'

'Yeah, a beautiful girl who likes the Stones.'

She smiled and looked at the floor. 'Thank you,' she said, almost blushing. She looked him directly in the eyes and he melted. Suddenly everything was gone – the bar, the people, the music. It was just him and her, until…

'Where the fuck have you been?' said a voice. Andy looked around to find Rick standing behind him. '

Sorry mate, I lost track of time.'

'Jesus, we've done half our set. You could've let me know you were here,' Rick grumbled.

'Can we talk about it later?' Andy gave Rick a look that said, 'kind of in the middle of something here, mate'. Rick, unimpressed, gave Tess the once over with his eyes.

'Has he told you he's got a micro-penis?' he said to her making a gesture with his little finger. Andy was speechless. Rick smiled at them both, gave Tess a cheeky wink and squeezed Andy's shoulder before heading back to the dressing room. 'Enjoy the rest of the show.'

'Friend of yours?' Tess asked.

'Unfortunately,' said Andy. 'Sorry about that – he's my flatmate.'

'Wow, you live with the lead singer of Four Zero?'

'I do.'

'My friend Lucy fancies the ass off him. That's why we're here.'

'I could always arrange an introduction for her.'

'Yeah, she'd really like that.'

'I think we're having a few drinks at our flat later, if you and your friend want to come.' She smiled at him, 'Yeah, that sounds good.' Oh yes, Andy thought – this was shaping up to be a great night.

'HELLO DIAMONDS!' Rick called out from the stage to a thunderous cheer from the crowd.

'Do you know what songs they're playing?' asked Tess as they both turned to the stage.

'Not sure.'

'WE'RE GONNA DO A FEW MORE SONGS FOR YOU TONIGHT – WE GOT ANY GUNS AND ROSES FANS IN?' Rick yelled, and the place erupted. 'OK, WE'RE GONNA PLAY A LITTLE SONG ABOUT WAR!'

Here we go, thought Andy. For all his faults there was no denying Rick was a natural showman and had a way of turning the crowd into anything he wanted them to be.

'EARLIER THIS YEAR WE ILLEGALLY INVADED A SOVEREIGN NATION!' More applause and screams from the crowd. 'THE FASCISTS IN LONDON AND WASHINGTON WANT US TO BELIVE THE LIES!' The cheers got louder. 'I SAY NO! I SAY "FUCK BLAIR!"' The cheers and applause were deafening. '...AND I SAY "FUCK BUSH!"' Andy thought the roof was going to come down. 'WE DON'T WANT IT!' He was working them all into a frenzy, and from his tone one would have thought they were going to play a fast, heavy rock song, but Andy knew different.

'THIS NEXT SONG'S CALLED *CIVIL WAR*.' He was manipulating the crowd, building up the emotion, building up the excitement. Now every pair of eyes in the place, including the doorman and bar staff, were fixed on Rick.

Then the band started playing. The soft strum of an acoustic guitar, then Rick whistling softly into the microphone. And he started to sing the first verse; the lyrics about how war was wrong and how all wars are civil wars, because human beings are fighting human beings.

After the fist verse he upped the volume, so he was almost shouting. At the exact same moment his voice went up, the electric guitars kicked in with the slow, powerful riff and a wave of electricity ran round the room. It made the hairs on Andy's neck stand on end, and by the look of them, it had the same effect on everyone else as well.

The crowd were hypnotised and hanging on his every word. It was the combination of music, heat, alcohol – the whole atmosphere. The audience was in Rick's pocket, and at that moment they would have believed anything he said as gospel.

This was power – real power. Rick must feel like a god. Three thousand people hanging on his every word. Andy even saw some girls faint. It was mass hypnosis. Andy felt Tess move her hand into his. OK, this is nice. He smiled on the inside and they watched Rick and the band finish the song together. The raw emotion that filled the room was tangible and the screams and shouts of applause seemed loud enough to burst eardrums. Tess leaned into Andy's ear. 'Why are they called Four Zero?'

Andy smiled, 'It's their new name, they used to be called Fuck Pussy.'

'Really? Why did they change it?'

Andy leaned in closer. 'Rick's brother's in the army. He's in Iraq right now and four zero is the call sign of his tank.' He spoke into her ear, drinking in her perfume and the smell of her hair. His lips were achingly close to hers. The applause gradually died down, and Rick was addressing the crowd again.

'THANK YOU. WE'RE GONNA SPEED THINGS UP A LITTLE NOW. THIS NEXT SONG IS BY A LITTLE BAND CALLED DEF LEPPARD. *ROCK OF AGESSS*!'

Tess turned her face close to Andy's and looked at him with those perfect eyes. 'Do you want to dance?'

'Sure.'

Tess led Andy by the hand to the dance floor, weaving between the hot dancing bodies. The serious emotion of the last song had been replaced by a happy, upbeat mood and the crowd were loving it.

Andy put his arms round Tess's perfectly toned waist, she put hers around his neck and they began to dance. She gyrated her hips against his pelvis and he moved his hands downwards – and she let him keep them there. From the stage Rick was could see everything, and he caught Andy's eye. Rick raised his eyebrows in approval and smiled then went to the other end of the stage, throwing himself into the chorus. Tess's lips met Andy's in a long, drawn-out kiss. As they felt the contours of each other's bodies, Andy felt impossibly happy.

The rest of the night passed by in a flash. Rick and the band finished their set and he and Rick joined Tess and her friends at their table. Andy and Tess held hands or had their arms round each other all night, just to keep touching each other. It felt natural – comfortable and right.

Once introduced, Rick and Tess's friend Lucy quickly found each other's tongues, and at the end of the evening the four of them headed back to Rick and Andy's flat.

Andy poured drinks and true to form, Rick brought out the coke. He hoovered a line off the coffee table and sat back into the sofa. Lucy seemed happy with this and did the same. Andy and Tess simply sat, locked in each other's arms, breaking away only for an occasional drink.

'So Tess, tell us about yourself,' Rick prompted. 'What makes you tick?'

Tess smiled. 'Why so interested?'

'That guy's my best mate,' he said, pointing to Andy. 'If your gonna be here longer than one night, I need to know your not gonna mess him about.'

'Awwww, the big tough rock star has a soft spot.' Her words were heavy with ridicule, but Rick was unfazed.

'I do. It's what makes me so great. Seriously though, what you into?'

Tess laughed and looked at Andy who just rolled his eyes. 'OK' she said, 'I'm studying English and journalism.'

'Why?' It was Rick's turn to lay on the ridicule.

'I like words. I love the power of the written word and everything it can do.'

'And what can it do?'

'Anything! Words can make you feel happy, sad – they can make you laugh or cry. They can change the way you think. Good writing's like music – surely you of all people must get that.'

Rick said nothing for a few moments. He was either deep in thought or the chemicals in his bloodstream had caught up with him.

'Bullshit,' he said, finally.

'You don't think so?' she challenged. Rick leaned forward and ran his fingers through his hair. 'So your theory is that words are like music? Explain.' he said.

'Do we really have to do this?' said Andy.

'It's all right,' Tess said to Andy, but looking straight at Rick. 'Take a novel, for instance. Words can take you to any time, any place – even inside the mind. And yes, good prose is like music – it can lift you up or bring you down, and that, my friend, is powerful and special!'

'If life was a novel it would make no sense whatsoever,' Rick insisted.

'What d'you mean?'

'In a novel there are rules,' he said, 'The main character has to grow – to go on a journey and discover something about themselves – and at the end they have to be a different person from at the beginning.'

'Right, so?'

'So, life isn't like that. There are millions – no fucking billions – of people on this planet who don't change at all, who don't grow – don't discover themselves. They simply grow up and do nothing – then they die, without doing anything worth remembering.'

Andy cut in. 'I don't agree, mate. It would have to be a pretty cold bastard – no, a very evil person – who when they died no one shed a tear. Everyone's loved by someone and therefore remembered, no matter what.'

'Fuck that,' said Rick, the chemicals now taking over completely. 'The world's fucked. People are fucked.' He stood up. 'Speaking of which…' and he grabbed Lucy's arm and led her off into his bedroom, to her evident delight.

Andy and Tess were left alone. 'Sorry about him.'

'It's OK. Lucy's not much better.'

They started to kiss again – but now it was more intense, more passionate. Andy gently kissed Tess's neck and moved down to her shoulder. They both knew what was coming. 'Do you want to see my Stones poster?' Andy asked. As soon as the words left his he mouth he heard how juvenile they sounded. Tess smiled as she kissed him. 'Yeah, I'd like that.'

They held hands as they made their way to Andy's room. He flicked on the light and immediately regretted it. This was a teenager's bedroom. He started to move things out of the way, he cleared the bed so they could at least sit down, and when he turned round, there she was, in her underwear. He took off his t-shirt and slowly walked over to her as she removed her bra. They kissed again, this time with the soft feel of each other's skin between them. They got into bed and made love for the first time.

When it was over they held each other and talked for what seemed like hours – about everything, about each other, their lives so far, their hopes and ambitions. Tess asked him how long the cup of tea had been on his bedside table, and he told her it had been there since just before he left the flat earlier. It hadn't moved or changed at all. It was exactly the same.

* * *

It had been love at first sight – though Andy wouldn't have believed it – and after both of them had graduated (a period doing what their grandparents would call 'courting'), Andy and Tess moved in together. They found a small two-bedroom semi to rent, both found jobs and life was good. They went to the cinema, out with friends, they ate out in restaurants and went on holiday at least once a year. They did all the things freedom brings.

They eventually got a mortgage and bought their own home, choosing their own furniture and spending their weekends in DIY stores. Then one day Tess announced she was pregnant.

Jake was born out of wedlock, but that didn't matter to Andy – they were happy.

It was two years later that Andy decided to propose – make it formal. Tess said yes, so Jake was two years old when he was a pageboy at his parents' wedding. His job was to carry the wedding rings down the aisle on a velvet cushion – it made him feel part of the big day.

On the day of the wedding, as family and friends gathered inside the church ready for the bride's arrival, Andy was in the parish office giving himself the once over in the full-length mirror with his father, who was acting as best man.

Andy's dad looked his son up and down, straightened his cravat and rubbed some fluff from his shoulder. 'Well, son, this is it.'

'I know, first day of the rest of my life.' He turned to his father and smiled.

'I'm very proud of you, Andrew.'

'I know, dad.'

'Me and your mum. Tess is a wonderful girl and Jake, well, he's a credit to you both.' He reached into his pocket. 'There's something I want you to have.' He pulled out a small metallic badge. 'This was your granddad's. He gave it to Andy who examined it, turning it over in his hand.

'It's his regimental cap badge from the war. Been to a few places, that has.'

'Dad, I, I don't know what to say. Thank you.'

'He gave it to me the day I married your mother. He said it was a good-luck charm, and now I'm giving it to you. Hopefully one day you'll give it to Jake on a day like this.'

Andy's eyes met his father's. 'Thanks, dad.'

'And it does bring some good luck. I've had that with me on every big day of my life, so if you want, you can do the same.'

'I will,' Andy said.

'I can't believe you're getting married. It seems only two minutes ago you were bouncing in my lap.' Andy could hear the lump forming in his father's throat. 'I'll give you a few minutes alone, son.'

'OK dad, and well… you know…'

'Yeah.' His father opened the office door and joined the waiting congregation.

Andy was alone; he turned back and looked at himself in the mirror. This is it, he thought. Your wedding day – and you're about to marry the girl of your dreams. What a lucky guy – some people search a lifetime for what you and Tess have, and now you're going to spend the rest of your lives together.

He took a deep breath… the rest of your lives. You're never going to sleep with anyone else. You're going to wake up every morning next to her. You are about to make a promise before God to love her for the rest of your days. You don't even believe in God, yet here you are in a church. Why? You were christened; you were raised in a Christian country. Easter. Christmas. Do you believe? No, you don't. Religion doesn't feature in your life, apart form the commercialised events that we call Christmas, Easter, and Valentine's Day. You don't pray. And you don't believe Jesus is actually our saviour. So why are you in a church?

Because that's what you do. The big white wedding. The christening of children. The burial of the dead. It's what we do. Why? Because it's what we do. It's what we've always done.

Together forever, for better or worse. 'Til death do you part. Andy took a deep breath, gave himself a last check to make sure nothing was out of place and made his way out to the pew in front of the altar, where in a few minutes he would make a promise before his family, his friends, and his god.

He took his place next to his father and waited for Tess to arrive. As he looked behind him, he saw all the people from all areas of his and Tess's lives – friends old and new, their extended family, work colleagues. This is your day – enjoy it.

The whole church rose as one as the organist struck up *Here Comes the Bride*. All heads turned to the back of the church to see Tess enter.

Andy's heart was in his mouth as he watched her walk down the aisle – she was a vision. As she got nearer his nervousness turned to pure happiness. He watched as Jake came down the aisle in front of his mother and smiled at him as he proudly gave his grandfather the rings he'd been carrying. The bridesmaids and ushers followed and took their places, then Tess took her place next to him. The organist stopped playing and there was silence as all eyes turned towards the priest.

'The grace of our Lord Jesus Christ, the love of God, and the fellowship of the Holy Spirit be with you,' he announced. A traditional Christian wedding service followed and the next thing Andy heard was the priest say 'I now pronounce you husband and wife, you may kiss the bride' His wedding was over. This was it. Married. Forever.

Now all thoughts turned to the rest of the day – the part of a wedding most people actually enjoyed – the eating and drinking and, for the single men, the time-honoured tradition of trying to sleep with a bridesmaid.

The congregation filed out of the church and threw confetti over Andy and Tess as the photographer set up for the different group photos.

After the photos, the guests made their way to the reception, and as the guests arrived, they filed past the bride and groom, shaking hands and offering their congratulations. Then, after the complementary glass of champagne came the three-course wedding breakfast.

Mellow from the wine, the guests sat back to hear the speeches from Tess's father, Andy and then the best man's speech. It was a classic, traditional wedding day. Andy and Tess took to the floor for the first dance, and gradually the rest of the guests started to join them.

The DJ played a mix of songs, old favourites and some current pop music, and as the music played and alcohol flowed the happy couple made the obligatory rounds, going from table to table to see all their guests – aunties, uncles, cousins, friends, colleagues. Some of them they saw every day, some once a year and some once in a blue moon – but there's nothing quite like a free meal to bring extended families and casual acquaintances together. Andy and Tess came to the table where they had put their old school and university friends, including Andy's one-time best friend, Rick, who had brought his brother as a guest. Fresh out of re-hab and on his best behaviour, Rick shook Andy's hand.

'Congratulations, mate.'

'Thanks mate. How you doing?' Rick shrugged his shoulders and tilted his head slightly. 'So so, mate.'

Andy hadn't seen Rick for a couple of years. They had drifted apart after university when Andy and Tess moved back to Manchester while Rick went to London to pursue a music career that sadly never took off. Rick was twenty years too late – rock was dead, or so all the agents and producers told him. So he performed as a tribute act, doing gigs in pubs and other small-time venues, but he still had a cocaine habit that could rival any multiplatinum artist, and this had brought him to The Priory clinic in London, his treatment paid for by his affluent family. This was the closest he ever got to being a rock star.

There was that awkward moment between Andy and Rick that happens when old friends meet who have lost touch – a hint of guilt and embarrassment. Guilt at not keeping in touch, and embarrassment because one of the two is usually doing better in life than the other.

'Glad to hear it,' said Andy. 'You'll have to come up some time, and we'll go out,' Andy continued.

'Yeah, that'll be good, mate.'

'All right then, see you in a bit.' And Andy and Tess moved on to the next table.

Towards the end of the night the DJ started to wrap things up – there was the old Sinatra chestnut, *New York, New York*, with everyone on the dance floor, then Andy and Tess said goodnight. They were booked into the hotel's honeymoon suite, and they left to cheers and wolf-whistles from the Andy's mates.

Andy and Tess went to bed with every intention of officially consummating their marriage, but a long day, rich food and lots of alcohol combined with a honeymoon suite that just wouldn't stop spinning put paid to their plans. Official consummation of the marriage would have to wait until the honeymoon. They fell asleep, drunk and happy. It had been a good wedding. Their wedding. A good day.

It had been a very expensive day that had been nine months in the planning and all in all had cost thirty thousand pounds – ten from Andy's parents, ten from Tess's family, with the happy couple finding the other ten. They had five thousand pounds in savings and a five thousand pound bank loan. They both thought it was worth it for their special day… they felt they'd got a bargain – their wedding was cheaper than a degree.

* * *

As the years passed Andy and Tess settled into married life – they worked on their home and enjoyed their son growing up. Then Tess fell pregnant again – Maggie arrived and they were a complete family.

Andy got restless in his job and started to look for another – that paid more money – because, as we've all been told, with money comes freedom. He signed up to several recruitment websites, some for his line of work and some not, but mostly he wanted to advance his career in advertising. It was what he enjoyed, and he didn't want to be one of those people that dreaded going to work every morning.

He applied for a few jobs, but got nowhere – until one day he received an email from one of the recruitment sites that dealt with the advertising industry. There was a job opening at Cheetham and Grant, one of the largest firms outside of London, based in Manchester. Andy had always wanted to work there, so the job was perfect and he applied for it straight away.

Then came the wait. He tried not to think about it – not to get his hopes up too high – but he couldn't help it. Getting this job would be so great. He checked his emails constantly, hoping for the offer of an interview. A few weeks past and he'd given up on it. If they'd not been in touch by now they obviously weren't interested. Then one day he checked his email and there, in his inbox, was an email from the HR manager at

Cheetham and Grant –with an invitation for an interview. Andy was over the moon.

On the morning of the interview he put on his new suit – more expensive than his usual work suits – bought especially for this day. He kissed Tess and the children goodbye and made the ten-minute walk to the train station. He'd already decided that if he got the job he'd commute by train into the city centre, as traffic was a nightmare. Today would be good practice. He carried a small rucksack containing his CV and references, along with his iPod, a book, a can of deodorant and some aftershave.

He made the station with fifteen minute to spare and bought his ticket, baulking at the price of a return, and made his way to the platform. He bought some mints and picked up a copy of *The Metro* from the kiosk on the platform and waited for his train.

He scanned through the paper, hoping to take his mind off the interview ahead, and quickly realised that free newspapers are free for a reason. He put it down and started to play with his phone, pretending to be doing something so as not to seem to sit and do nothing. You couldn't just sit and wait patiently anymore – you had to be doing something – texting, calling, playing with an app. Modern people were far to busy, important and interesting to just sit and do nothing while waiting for a train, a bus, a doctor's appointment. Anything. If you did you might actually have to have a conversation with someone.

Andy's train arrived on time and he and a dozen others squeezed into the already brim full carriages. The term 'standing room only' was an understatement – there was only just breathing room. There was something about being able to a smell a stranger's clothes that made Andy uncomfortable. How is it that being surrounded by people can be one of the loneliest places on earth?

The train made three stops before the city centre. The people gradually disembarked and headed to their offices and work. Andy was swept along in the tide of people as he too made his way out of the station and got his bearings.

The offices of Cheetham and Grant were a ten-minute walk away and as he got nearer the butterflies in his stomach grew increasingly restless. What if he messed up? Embarrassed himself? Said the wrong thing? Come on, he thought. Stop it. Self esteem, man. Confidence. You are the right man for the job. Do it.

He arrived at the plush offices and a short journey in the lift brought him to the main reception. He checked in at the desk and took a seat, waiting nervously to be called to the interview. He was to meet the HR manager and one of the partners, who also happened to be the eldest son of one of the founders. A secretary appeared and called him to follow her… this was it.

The interview went well – very well. They said they'd be in touch and shook hands – and Andy was once again on the streets of the city. He stopped off for a bite to eat a bistro – an overly pricey ham and cheese panini and a bottle of coke slipped down nicely before making his way back to the station.

The same journey in reverse. Like rewinding videotape, only with significantly less people. He arrived back at home and found himself at a loss – Andy wasn't used to being home during the day. Tess would be picking the kids up from school and nursery as usual so he didn't have anywhere to be. With time on his hands he opened the laptop. There was new website Tess had joined and Andy soon followed. It was called Facebook – they called it a 'social network' – a website where you had 'friends' and could interact with each other. Everyone had a profile page where you could upload photos and the details your life – your job, home town, relationship status. This last made Andy smile – if only they'd had this when he was at uni. You could even share your religion or political views. He scrolled through his news feed to see what was going on. The answer, of course, was nothing. If any of his real friends had big news or something was happening, he'd get a phone call – on the other hand, the appeal of announcing something big on Facebook was understandable, you get to tell everyone in your life at the same time. At least you'd save on the phone bill...

After checking Facebook, Andy went to iTunes and one song turned into five. Then he found himself drooling over images of Aston Martins that he could neither afford nor, if he owned up, be able to use. Hard to do the family shop or the school run in a two-seater. He spent several hours browsing and only got up from the couch to put the kettle on as Tess and the children arrived home.

There followed the usual routine of getting in, taking off coats, sorting bags, lunch boxes and homework and communications from the school, getting drinks, and it was a while before Andy and Tess could talk over the events of the day. By seven thirty the children were tucked up in bed – the evening was theirs. Tess relaxed watching TV soaps while Andy read – he was a few chapters into *Ulysses* and finding it heavy going when the phone rang – not a mobile but the landline – which was strange. No-one ever called the landline these days, apart from sales and marketing cold calls. Have you had an accident? Do you want to claim against mis-sold ppi? Do you want to change your energy supplier? It had become so intrusive that generally Andy and Tess would let it go to the answering machine, and this time was no different. The ringing stopped and they heard in the background the familiar buzz click of the answering machine recording. Usually the call centres left no message so all they heard was static.

'Hi Andy, it's Mike, Rick's brother. Can you call me back as soon as you get this message? Thanks.'

Andy and Tess both looked at each other, they were both thinking the same thing, that he'd fallen of the wagon again.

Andy got up and went to the phone. 'This should be good.' He dialled 14713 to return the call. The phone rang just five times before Mike answered.

'Hi Andy, thanks for getting back to me so soon.'

'What's up?'

'I've got some bad news, mate. There's no easy way to say it…'

'Rick?'

'Yeah. They found him this morning.'

Numbness crawled through Andy. His grip on the phone tightened slightly. As Mike gave him more details, he glanced over at Tess who hadn't taken her eyes off him. She knew, and as the conversation unfolded she put her hand over her mouth and began to sob.

Eventually Andy put the phone down, completely at a loss as to what he could do or say. He ran his hands over his face and went to hold Tess – to try to comfort her.

'Are you all right?' she ventured.

'Yeah… The shock… but we always knew…'

'Yeah…' She kissed him on the cheek.

'I need a drink. Do you want one?'

'No, I'm OK, thanks.'

Andy went into the kitchen and from the top cupboard where they kept the booze pulled down a bottle of Jack Daniels he'd been given by a client at Christmas. He didn't normally drink spirits but he felt this situation called for something a little stronger than beer.

He found a tumbler and a can of cola from the fridge. Trying to open the bottle of Jack Daniels with his shaking hands was a task in itself. He fiddled about with the plastic seal, trying to peel it back with his fingernail. To no avail. He got a small knife and managed to prise the seal off.

He stared at the bottle – the shape, the black label with its white lettering in an old fashioned typeface. Number seven. The golden liquid it held within – the whole thing was pure rock and roll. He unscrewed the cap and poured a three-finger measure into the glass. He took a long sniff at the top of the bottle before putting the lid back on, then he opened the can of cola and filled the rest of the glass. He took a sip. It was strong – but it was good. As he took another, larger sip he felt a lump in the back of his throat and a stinging behind his eyes. Suddenly the tears were streaming down his cheeks, and he fought to get his breath, forcing him to put the glass down.

He felt the embrace of Tess arms around him. 'It's OK, Andy,' she said. 'I know he was one of your closest friends for a long time.'

Andy wiped the tears away as Tess let go. 'I know, it's just that he's dead. Dead.'

The rest of the night and the following few days passed in a blur.

Andy and Tess tried to carry on as normal until Andy received another phone call from Rick's brother, Mike. He could go and see Rick in the chapel of rest if he wanted.

The drive to Rick's hometown was only an hour, and the family had decided to bury him there rather than in London. Andy was torn, he wanted to say goodbye to him properly, but the thought of seeing him dead made his blood run cold. When Andy was a boy he went to see his grandmother in the chapel of rest, and it had scared him. It wasn't his nana in the coffin – it was someone else. It looked like the woman he knew, but that was all. The woman he knew wasn't there.

It was Tess who insisted that he go and see Rick – it would help him with the grieving process. So he went. The drive was uneventful and as Andy pulled into the small car park next to the undertaker's premises, he became nervous. What would he be like? Would he be the Rick he remembered or would it be the same as his nana?

He rang the undertaker's bell and waited to be ushered in. A small elderly woman let Andy in and he told her whom he had come to see. After he had signed the visitor's sheet, she led him down a corridor and stopped outside an ominous-looking white door with an ornate gold handle. In the middle of the door, just above eye level, was a gold number five.

'Here we are,' she said in a soft, low voice, gently opening the door as if not to disturb the occupant inside. The door opened painfully slowly and Andy rocked back and forth on from his toes to his heel, feeling the thick plush carpet beneath his shoes.

The old lady smiled returned to the reception area, leaving Andy alone. For a few seconds he stood frozen in the doorway, taking in his surroundings – the room was beautiful. The lighting was low and Andy stepped over the threshold, shutting the door very gently behind him. On the other side of the room with a chair at its foot.

He felt strange sense of unnaturalness – something surreal. Andy walked over to the coffin just as he did when he checked on the kids at night –gently, quietly, softly. But instead of a sleeping child at rest, the form that met his eyes was the empty shell of a dead drug addict. For a brief moment Andy recoiled in horror and revulsion. Thin, gaunt, waxy – this wasn't his friend. This wasn't the guy who could command a stage and the attention of thousands of strangers. This was grotesque.

Andy didn't know what to do. He wanted to go, to get away from this thing, but he forced himself to look again upon the face of his former friend. He wanted to tell him all the things he never got a chance to say, and to tell him he was sorry for not staying in touch after uni – that he was sorry his life turned out the way it did. Andy sat down on the chair. 'I'm sorry I wasn't there for you, mate,' he said in a whisper. 'I hope wherever you are you've found peace.'

Time to get out of there. He walked to the door and put his hand on the handle, but paused and turned back to the coffin. 'Enjoy the great gig in the sky, mate. Goodbye.'

Andy closed the door gently behind him and made his way to where the old lady was sitting at the reception. 'Thank you,' he said.

'Would you like to sign the book of condolence?'

'No – no thank you.' He left the building and went back to the car. On the drive home he listened to Guns and Roses' greatest hits.

A few days later Andy found himself making the same drive back to Rick's hometown for the funeral. The mourners would gather at Rick's parents house, ready for the undertaker to arrive with the hearse, then there would be the procession where family and friends followed the hearse and funeral car to the church in a sombre convoy.

Andy had always known Rick's family had money, but it was something they never talked about. As he pulled up outside the house Andy realised that his friend's parents must be millionaires – they had to be with a house that big. Must be a least seven bedrooms. He parked a little further down the road and walked over to the small crowd gathered at the edge of the drive. He immediately picked out Mike by the army uniform and chestful of medals, and at the same time Mike saw Andy and went over to him. 'Andy, glad you could make it,' he said shaking his hand.

'How are you, Mike?'

'So so. Be glad when today's over.'

'Yeah, me too.'

'How's the family?'

'Good, doing well'

'Can you stay for the wake or do you have to get back home?'

'No, I'll come back for a bit.'

'Good stuff. I'll catch up with you later – we'll have a drink for my brother.' Mike walked away to greet someone else.

The hearse duly arrived and led the funeral on the long, slow drive to the chapel. Then the usual ceremony – pallbearers taking the coffin in, the priest offering words of comfort. Mike stood up and gave the eulogy and his uncle read a suitable passage from *The Bible*. Ironic, given that at university

Rick had hated religion and was a devout atheist. 'Fairy tales for the weak-minded and ignorant', he called it. Andy found himself wondering what an atheist funeral would look and sound like. He glanced over to Rick's parents every now and then – his mum could scarcely hold it together throughout the service, while his father tried to comfort her and stay strong. Even millions of pounds can't shield you from the darkness of this world – or guarantee happiness.

The service came to an end and as Motley Crue's *Home, Sweet Home* was piped through speakers into the chapel, the curtains in front of the coffin closed. His friend was gone

Throughout the service so many good words were spoken about Rick. To hear it all one would have thought he was a saint. No one said a word about how he died. Drugs weren't ever mentioned – nor was his arrogance or his temper. Why is it we only say good things about the dead, forgetting the harsh realities? Where did that come from, 'You should never speak ill of the dead' or 'god rest 'em'? Was it because deep down we all know we'll end up there one day – and we'd want the same respect given to us? Or was it because in the end, the good side and finer qualities of a person stand out and that's what we want to remember? People are strange.

The family had chosen cremation, so there was no graveside farewell, so after the service everyone headed back to Ricks parents' house. The usual scenario, everyone standing around awkwardly, explaining to people how they knew the deceased, swapping stories and anecdotes and, of course toasting their passing with alcohol.

Andy felt uncomfortable and out of place at Rick's parents' house. The other mourners were not from his world. They were mostly members of Rick's family – all very upper class – the only thing they had in common being Rick himself. He doubted anyone wanted to hear stories about what they got up to at university. The only person Andy knew at all was Mike, as they'd been on a few nights out together, but he was busy doing the rounds, being the dutiful son and making sure everyone was looked after.

Andy chatted briefly with one of the guys from Rick's old band, Four Zero. Andy didn't recognise him at first – he was an accountant now with a wife and family.

Andy was preparing to make an exit and say his goodbyes when Mike came over. 'Are you off now?' he asked.

'Yeah, why?' said Andy.

'I thought we could have a drink and catch up.'

'I'd love to mate, but I'm driving.'

'Why don't you stay over? Christ knows we've got the room – plus my mum and dad will be going to bed as soon as everyone leaves.'

Andy thought about it – he'd have to let Tess know. 'Yeah, OK. Why not?' He called Tess and she was fine about it – she understood.

As the afternoon turned into evening and people started to drift away, Mike showed Andy to the room he'd be staying in. He didn't felt a little uncomfortable that he didn't have a change of clothes or any toiletries, but sod it, it was only one night and he'd be home in the morning. He wanted to give his friend a good send-off – and what better way to do it than have a few drinks with the brother he'd so idolised.

'This is you mate,' said Mike opening the door to a guest bedroom.

'Right. OK, think I'll be fine here.' Andy couldn't help noticing that this bedroom was bigger than the entire downstairs of his house.

'Come on, let's have a drink.' As they walked across the landing, Andy stopped outside one of the doors, on which was displayed a poster that he knew very well. It was a copy of the sign outside Area 51 in America, telling people to keep out and that deadly force was authorised. Andy had seen and walked past that same poster every day at university – Rick had put it up on the outside of his bedroom door in the flat they shared. And now it was here, in his parents' house. 'That's his room,' said Mike. 'Well, was…'

'He had that poster in the flat at uni…'

'Do you want to take a look inside?' Mike offered. 'Go in if you want, it's Rick all over, that room.'

Andy hesitated for moment, part of him felt uncomfortable at the notion and part of him was curious. 'Yeah, I will if you don't mind.'

'Roger. I'll go get us some drinks. What you having?'

'Just a beer please.'

'Sorry, no beer tonight, mate – only the hard stuff,' Mike smiled.

'All right then, a Jack and coke if you've got it.' Mike was already on his way downstairs. 'The size of this house? What do you think?' Mike said laughingly, without turning round.

Andy took a deep breath and went into Rick's room. The light from the landing cast an eerie glow across his friend's sanctum – and from the looks of it, that what it was – his inner sanctum. Andy flicked on the light. It was clear that Rick had spent a lot of time in this room. It seemed funny how someone's whole life can be encapsulated in one room. It struck Andy that it must have been very lonely for him. In the end, after all his bullshit and front, all Rick ever wanted was to be loved. Isn't that what we all want?

Andy didn't want to be in that room any longer, and he made to leave – but something on the chest of drawers caught his eye. A photo. He picked it up and was overcome with sadness and guilt. It was of him and Rick at university, in their first year. Rick had his arm round him. They were both smiling – and both drunk. Andy couldn't believe he'd kept it all these years. He placed the photo back down and walked out, taking one last look at what remained of his friend's life before turning off the light and closing the door.

He walked downstairs and joined Mike in the living room, – or 'drawing room', as they called it. Mike gave him his drink, 'Sit down mate.'

'Thanks.' Andy took a seat on a sofa and Mike sat opposite him on another one, the other side of a large antique oak table. Mike loosened his tie – he was still in his uniform, and Andy's eyes were drawn to the medals on his chest. He counted five.

'To Rick,' Mike announced, raising his glass.

'To Rick,' Andy echoed and they both took a gulp. 'So, when do you have to go back to the barracks?'

'I've got a couple of weeks to go yet. They're quite good for stuff like this.' Mike changed the subject. 'So, how's the family? You got two kids now, right?'

'Yeah, a boy and a girl.'

They talked and drank for hours. Andy told Mike about his life and Mike did the same. He was divorced, no kids. A career soldier, he lived and breathed the army and as the night wore on and the drink flowed Andy built up the courage to ask him something that had been on his mind since they first met years ago. 'Can I ask you something, mate?'

'Yeah, sure, anything'

'What's it like?'

'What?'

'You know… war,' said Andy almost slurring his words. Mike laughed and nearly choked.

'What do you want to know?' Mike was smiling. Andy thought about it – he didn't really know what to ask.

'Is it scary?' he said.

Mike stopped smiling and suddenly became serious. 'Yeah' he said taking another drink. 'Yeah, it's scary.' Andy didn't know what to say.

'Sorry mate, I…'

'It's OK,' said mike. 'The truth is that war is ninety per cent boredom and ten per cent sheer terror. And in films and on TV and computer games they only show you the ten per cent, and not the other ninety. Be a pretty poor film if they did.'

'I don't get it,' Andy said, a little confused. 'How can war be boring?'

'Because most of the time you're waiting for something to happen. You're either waiting for something or moving to another place where you wait for something to happen.'

'I still don't get it.'

'Think of it like a roller coaster. You queue up for a long time. Then you get in the ride. You strap yourself in and then finally you set off. But the bit you queued up for hasn't happened yet. You have to go up the hill.' Mike raised his arm and pointed straight upwards to make the point.

'Right, OK.'

'So you're going up the hill – you know what's going to happen. Everyone with you knows what's going to happen. And it takes forever. And you get closer and closer to the drop.' Mike paused.

'And then you drop?' Andy ventured.

'Yeah, you drop. And for the next ninety seconds or so you're terrified. And then it's over. Just like that. And you're back to where you started. Only in a war, you have to go through that two or three times a day.'

'Have you ever killed anyone?'

'I have.' And before Andy could respond Mike continued, 'I've been a professional soldier for fifteen years. I've done tours of Northern Ireland, Kosovo. I fought in the Iraq war and went back twice. I've done three tours of Afghanistan. In that time I've killed eleven men. I took the lives of eleven people – real, flesh and blood people. I've had four men die under my command, two to enemy and fire and two to

IED strikes. But do you know what bothered me the most during all that?'

'No.' Andy was becoming slightly uncomfortable at the way the conversation had turned.

'The thing that upset me the most – when it happened,' said Mike, 'was the cows.'

'The cows?'

'Yeah, the bloody cows,' said Mike, half smiling. 'Yes, I've lost blokes and I've taken lives – that will stay with me forever. Those memories are never going to go away. But at the time it all happened I had a job to do, you know. I didn't have time to get upset and dwell on it then and there. I do now, Jesus I do now. But them fucking cows really got to me.'

'Mate with the greatest respect, I haven't got a clue what your talking about.' Mike laughed, and so did Andy.

'The foot and mouth outbreak, you muppet,' said Mike.

'Ah, right' Andy said. 'You had to do that?'

'Yeah, I was fresh out of training and had just arrived at the unit. I tell you mate, seeing all those cows burning in a big fucking pile really got to me. It was so sad. And they knew – they fucking knew what was going to happen to them. You could see it in their eyes. It was so sad. Mike took another long drink. 'Like I said, at the time it happened – but now though it doesn't bother me. But the other stuff…'

'Yeah mate, I can only imagine,' said Andy. 'For what it's worth I think you're a fuckin' hero.' Andy raised his glass to Mike.

'I'm no hero, mate, just did my job. I was scared shitless most of the time, just like everyone else. What makes me laugh is that I volunteered for it. But I'll tell you this, if every single politician and elected official and world leader had served on the frontline in a combat zone and fired their weapon in anger under contact with the enemy, war would be a thing of the past in a matter of hours. It would be consigned to the history books as something mankind used to do, like slavery. We all find the concept of slavery abhorrent in this day and age, but it was accepted as normal once upon a time. And I hope one day we can say the same about war.'

'I don't know what I'd do in a war,' Andy mused. 'I don't know if I could find the strength. I'd probably shit myself.'

'You do what you have to – and you never know your true strength until you've been tested.'

'Yeah, I suppose so.'

They had a couple more large drinks before turning for the night.

The next morning, with a hangover from hell, Andy said his goodbyes to Rick's parents and Mike.

As he drove home he thought how much he wanted a shower and a change of clothes. It was Saturday, so the kids would be at home, and a much-needed nap was out of the question.

Tess and Maggie were sitting together on the couch when he walked in, smiling at him.

'What?' he said. Then from behind the door Jake jumped out and shot him with a water pistol.

'Bang, bang! You're dead, dad!' he shouted, to uncontrolled laughter from Tess and Maggie.

'Ha ha, very funny.' Andy wiped his face dry.

'Stick 'em up, dad,' Jake ordered, pointing the water pistol in Andy's face.

Andy closed his eyes and heard Tess say, 'You're dead, Andy. Give it up.'

But then, when he opened his eyes, Andrew Baker wasn't at home having fun with his family. He was in London. In a skyscraper. Stuck in a lift with the barrel of a gun pointed at his head.

He heard the loud, sickening click of Khalid pulling the hammer back. Andy was terrified. He wanted to go home. He wanted to see Tess and the kids. He didn't have the strength for this. It seemed that time itself had slowed down. Andy could feel the cold barrel against his skin.

He's going to kill me, he thought. This terrorist is going to kill me. Andy's heart was thumping, faster and faster, his hands were sweaty and he was shaking. He couldn't move if he wanted to.

The only thought going through his mind was, I don't want to die, I don't want to die, I don't want to die.

13

The Four Freedoms Tower rose above the London skyline, a symbol of what could be achieved. Intended to be the tallest structure on earth, it was built on a site that meant when it was completed, the tower would be visible from any route into the city. Designed by a firm of award-winning architects, the Four Freedoms was to become the jewel in the London property crown – duplex apartments with a hefty seven-figure price tag and all the mod cons that a wealthy individual could want.

Most of the apartments were already sold before the ground had even been prepared. The investors and architects toasted their own brilliance and patted each other on the back. It was all about the money. For the human race it had been about money for centuries – wealth and materialism. Money and greed had taken over heaven many moons ago. Money was the new god and everyone was a convert. Then it all came crashing down – a metaphor so ironic it bordered on farce.

The same investors and moneymen that loaned the money to the owners had also been lending money to everybody else. Even those who could not pay it back. Then the bubble burst – recession, worldwide – which meant that instead of a playground for the rich, the Four Freedoms Tower became the largest tenement block ever built. It also meant that by the time the building was ready to be fitted out on the inside, there was no money left for details such as CCTV cameras, biometric entry system and security systems in the lifts. Everything was done on a shoestring with contracts awarded to the lowest bidder. But in building, as in life, you get what you pay for.

So instead of eight lifts, as originally planned, there were only four, to service a building that probably had over three thousand people in it at any given time.

Now, in the darkness of the lift shaft, the cable suspending Andy and Khalid a few hundred feet above the ground was damaged and began to fray. Normally this would not have been a problem – there were back ups and emergency brakes that would stop the lift should the cable give way – but these measures were automatic and controlled by a computer.

And computers never, ever, stop working.

14

Bob the concierge gripped the telephone until his knuckles turned white. 'You're gonna be another forty minutes? That's outrageous... Right, I'll see you in a bit.'

He put the phone down and rubbed his eyes as if he were a stockbroker that had lost a billion.

'Bloody engineers,' he muttered.

Before he could return to his laptop, he was surprised by a loud banging on the glass entrance door. He took a look at the CCTV monitor and saw four men – two of them in police uniform. He pressed the button on the console to open the doors, and the men strode purposefully to his desk. Bob noticed how attractive the man who seemed to be in charge was. Stop it, he thought to himself, he's half your age.

'Good morning, gents. What can I do for...?' but before Bob could finish, the man in plain clothes held up a police badge and Bob's heart sank, and his thoughts turned to the phone call he'd received before.

'I'm Inspector Taylor. We have reason to believe that somewhere in this building is a man who is planning a terrorist attack. We spoke on the phone earlier. Now, here's my ID, now let's have some co-operation.'

Bob was overwhelmed by a combination of fear and embarrassment. The call had been real. How was he to know? They got crank calls all the time. A terrorist in the building… Jesus. He thought of Jimmy and the dogs and all the people sleeping in the apartments above him.

'Yes sir no problem. What was his name again?'

'We only know him as Khalid – roughly twenty, twenty-five years old, a student. Here take a look.' the inspector handed Bob a photograph.

As he looked at the photo Bob's stomach churned and his heart began to race.

'Fuck me. Yeah. He lives here, all right. A nice fella too, always smiling.' The concierge couldn't take his eyes off the image in his hand.

'Which apartment?' said the inspector, breaking the photo's spell.

'Oh, right. Floor 50, apartment 5.'

The inspector took back the photo and looked round.

'Thank you. Where are the lifts?'

Overcome by embarrassment, Bob could say only, 'Sorry sir, but one of the lifts is stuck.'

The inspector simply shrugged his shoulders, not fully understanding what Bob meant. 'So what – a building this size presumably has more than one lift?'

'There are three, but when one gets stuck, the rest automatically come to the ground floor – for safety, you see.' The inspector didn't have time to inquire about the absurdity of this. He was running out of time and patience.

'Where are the stairs?'

'Over there sir. You'll need the key.' Bob turned to fetch it.

'Right, Jamie. You and these two stay here. You come with me,' he said to one of the uniformed officers.

Bob unlocked the door and they headed up the stairs. The inspector turned. 'Jamie, no-one comes in or out till you have heard from me.'

'No problem, boss.'

The inspector started to run up the stairs, the door closing sharply behind him.

15

Inside the lift Khalid's gun was pointing straight at Andy's head as the two men stared intently at each other. For what seemed like hours there was silence as sweat ran down both their faces. Then finally Khalid eased the hammer back down and lowered the pistol.

'You know Andy, you're right. Killing you now would only make my task harder. So instead I will change my intended target and when the lift doors open on the ground floor I will give, say, a ten-second head start and then I want you to run; run as fast as you can. Scream about what I am. Cause as much panic as possible before I complete my mission.'

The little courage Andy had managed to summon in confronting him disappeared, along with all hope he had of getting out unharmed. What could he do now?

'And… and… what if I try and stop you?'

'Ha. You won't. Do you know why? Like you said, you are not a solider. You are a coward and a weakling. And if you do try, my friend here will take care of you.' Khalid grinned malevolently as he flashed the gun at Andy, who shrank into the wall. There was silence again as Andy stared at the floor, trying desperately to think of what to do next. A million thoughts spun through his mind, a million memories. There must be something he could say to persuade this lunatic not to commit murder. There was nothing left. There was nothing else to do but one thing.

'Khalid,' he said, almost whispering.

'Yes, Andy.'

Pleadingly, Andy looked him in the eye. 'Please don't do this. There has be some other way.' Beyond control in this unnatural situation, he began to sob, tears pouring down his cheeks. The back of his throat burned and his stomach tightened.

'Look, there are people I work with back home who believe in the same god as you. They are nice people – good people and I don't for one second believe that they want me dead or hurt… So… so if they can tolerate our ways and live in the same place with us in peace, then…'

Khalid, his anger and hatred undiminished, got up and knelt next to Andy, pushing the barrel into the side of his head and shouting. 'Don't you dare, you fucking infidel. The people you speak of are traitors and they will see the error of their ways. They are betrayers.'

Khalid moved the gun from Andy's head and pushed it into his mouth.

'If I kill you now, who would care? Are you a nobody? Or do you have a family? Children? Answer me pig!'

'I… I have a wife and two children.'

'Your children – will they miss you? Will they cope, growing up without you; do you think they will visit your grave often?

Andy's eyes didn't move. Khalid got to his feet, pressing the barrel of the gun against his forehead. Andy looked up slowly towards Khalid.

'You know what. You are nothing but a modern Nazi! An extremist. There are people like you in all cultures and faiths. And just like the rest, you make one big mistake.'

'Oh, and what's that?'

'You mentioned the children!'

In a split second, Andy was on one knee and used every ounce of strength he had to punch Khalid square in the groin. As they struggled on the floor, the lift trembled around them.

16

'Hit him back, Josef, hit him back' he heard her say. Khalid was no longer in the lift at the Four Freedoms Tower. He wasn't fighting Andrew Baker. He wasn't on a holy mission for Allah – and his name was not Khalid. He was thirteen years old, and he was fighting Kurt. Or more accurately, being beaten up by Kurt.

Josef felt Kurt's fist smash into the side of his head, then his other fist slammed into his cheek. It was all happening so fast. Josef wasn't sure what was worse, the physical pain of being hit very hard in the face or the embarrassment of it being done in front of her. And after all it was because of her that he was fighting.

'Hit him Josef! Hit him back!' he heard Anna say. Anna was his best and only real friend, who lived on his street a few doors down. Her family moved in a few years ago and their parents became friends which led to Josef and Anna spending a lot of time together. They would play in the back garden in summer and in winter would retreat to Josef's bedroom. She was beautiful, not just to his eyes but his heart and soul as well. She accepted him unconditionally for who he was, and whenever something upset her and those perfect eyes shed tears of sorrow, Josef felt a fire and a rage so fierce it led him to a dark place. Like fighting the biggest boy in school after he had called Anna a vile name.

He felt Kurt's knee slam into his stomach. He couldn't breathe, and he fell to floor. The next thing he felt was a foot crash into his face. He was going to die – Kurt was going to beat him to death. From nowhere he heard another voice – one of the teachers. He was dragged to his feet and taken away. He could barely see straight and the next thing he knew he was in the school nurse's office. There was blood everywhere. He felt sick, either because of his wounds or at the sight of his own blood.

The school called his parents to collect him, and when Josef's mother saw the damage done to her only son's face she burst into tears. After some strong words with the headmaster, she took Josef home and sent him to bed to recover.

He lay in bed in that place between sleep and being awake. He could vaguely hear his mother's voice. 'Not today' she said, then, 'Soon.' Was she on the phone? Strange, he thought, as he drifted off to sleep.

He was woken by the sound of the front door, voices and then footsteps on the stairs. He wasn't sure how long he'd been asleep but it was still daytime. His bedroom door opened, and it was Anna. He wasn't sure why, but he kept his eyes closed, pretending to be asleep. She crept into his room, sat on the edge of the bed, and started to gently stroke his hair. It felt wonderful; he never wanted it to stop. 'Josef,' she whispered, and he opened his eyes. She smiled at him and ran her soft fingers down his cheek, 'Are you OK?'

'Fine,' whispered Josef, smiling painfully.

'That was very brave.'

'It's OK.'

'Thank you,' and she leaned in and kissed his forehead. Her beautiful face was inches away from his. They looked into each other's eyes and their lips met and their mouths opened. She put her tongue into his mouth. It felt very strange at first but then their tongues met and Josef felt something he had never felt before. She climbed into his bed and they kissed, and kissed, and kissed. His hands discovered her body and he felt her breasts as her hands found their way into his pyjamas.

As they caressed and kissed time itself slowed to a crawl – until they heard Josef's mother coming up the stairs. Anna leapt out of the bed and they just managed to compose themselves before the door opened. Josef's mother peered in. 'Time to go home, Anna, your mother's just called.'

'OK, Mrs Reiniger.' Anna got off the bed. 'Bye, Josef. See you soon.'

'Bye.'

'I'll see Anna out, then I'm going to make dinner before your father comes home. do you feel up to coming downstairs.'

'I'll stay up here, if that's ok?'

'Of course, sweetheart.' His mother and Anna left his room, and before the door closed he saw Anna turn and smile at him.

Josef spent the next few days Josef recovering from his injuries. He would spend the day anxiously waiting for Anna to come round after she had finished school, and then they would make excuses to go to his bedroom so they could be alone.

Now Josef had a girlfriend – albeit a secret one as they both decided to keep it a secret from their parents and their friends – he felt happy. Everything made sense when she was with him – was this love? He didn't know. All he knew was life was better because he had her.

Anna spent a lot of time Josef's house and one day they were sitting in his kitchen doing their homework while his mother prepared dinner.

'Oh, look, there's that cat again,' said Josef's mother. She went over to the window and looked out into the back garden.

'Where?' asked Josef, getting up to join her.

'Over there – look.'

Anna joined them at the window, 'Is that the cat you were telling me about?' she asked.

'Yes, it's been hanging around our garden for the past few days. My dad goes mental.' Josef said.

'Why?'

'Because it does its business on the lawn,' Josef's mother cut in. 'My husband is very protective of his lawn'

'Look, it's doing it again,' said Josef, half laughing.

The moment was interrupted by the phone ringing. 'Right, back to work you two.' His mother went to answer the phone and Anna and Josef returned to their homework. From the hallway they heard his mother.

'What? No, really? Right, I'll put it on'

Josef and Anna looked at each other. They heard his mother switch on the television in the living room and they got up to see what was going on.

They found his mother on the sofa, transfixed by events on the screen.

'What's going on mum? Who was on the phone?'

'It was your father, he said something's happened in America, and he asked if we were watching'

'What is it?' Josef asked.

'Look,' said his mother, pointing at the screen. He saw scenes from New York; smoke was billowing from a tall building.

'Is this real?' he said.

'Yes, it's the news.' His mother flicked through the channels, and it was on every station.

'My God,' Anna gasped, 'What's happened?'

They sat together on the sofa and watched the events as they unfolded. Another plane hit one of the towers. 'Oh, my God,' said Josef's mother in disbelief, covering her mouth with her hand.

'This is madness,' said Anna. 'Are there people inside?'

'Probably.' said Josef. 'Who would do this?'

As they watched history in the making, Josef felt Anna's hand creep into his. They held hands and watched the biggest terrorist attack in history. Gradually, more information emerged about who had done this and why, and Josef's mother began to cry. 'There's going to be a war,' she said. 'America will go to war over this.'

'With who?' said Josef.

'With everybody.'

'We wouldn't get involved though, would we, Mrs Reiniger?' asked Anna.

'I don't know… we might,' she said, 'but the British will.'

'Good, it might give them something to do other than cause trouble for us,' said Josef. 'They're all pigs anyway, drinking and fighting and driving like lunatics.'

'Stop it, Josef,' his mother warned.

'Why, it's true,' he said. 'Don't even know why they're still here. Not like Hitler or the Soviets are coming back anytime soon.'

'I SAID THAT'S ENOUGH!' said his mother, and both Josef and Anna were taken aback by her tone – she looked very upset. 'Just stop it.' And she got up and left the room, 'I'm going to make a phone call.'

'What was that about?' Anna asked.

'Don't know,' Josef shrugged.

They carried on watching the news, holding hands until Anna got up to go to the toilet. While she was gone Josef thought about what was happening in America. It was terrible and horrific. Thousands must be dead. It was genius. It was so simple – fly a plane into a building. How many bombs would it take to drop two tall skyscrapers? He remembered his father telling him how the British soldiers always use to look underneath their cars before they got in. The IRA had once blown up a soldier's car by planting a bomb underneath it, and when he put the key in the ignition it exploded. After that happened, all the British soldiers in Germany checked their cars before they got in. A good way to spread fear. But this – this was something else. This could happen anywhere, to anyone. It was one thing to read about terrorism in the newspaper – it was horrible but it wasn't real – it was somewhere else and happening to other people. This was different. Seeing it happen live on the news made it very real – watching the towers fall with thousands of people inside made it truly terrifying. And if they could do that to America, on American soil – if they could strike at the heart of the richest and most powerful nation on earth, they could do it anywhere.

And Josef didn't even know why. He wondered why someone would do this, but his thoughts were distracted by Anna coming back into the room. She sat down next to him again and held his hand.

As the news channel gave more information from America Anna turned to him, 'Who was your mother talking to on the phone? She was speaking English,' she said.

'What, English?'

'Yes, she was on the phone talking to someone in English.'

'Don't know, might be a friend. She used to work at a British barracks.'

'Oh right.' said Anna, and the matter was dropped.

They carried on watching the news until Josef's father came home and made them switch it off. 'That's enough of that,' he said. 'Terrible day. What is the world coming to?' he said as he left the room.

From the kitchen they heard his father shouting and swearing – he had evidently seen what the cat had left on the back lawn. As they ate dinner Josef's father was still complaining about the cat, much to Anna and Josef's amusement and his mother's annoyance.

'If I catch it, I'll string it up,' his father warned.

'Oh for goodness sake, will you stop talking about that cat?' said his mother irritably. 'There are more important things to be concerned about.'

'Like what?' said his father.

'Like what happened today'

'And why should we be concerned? There's nothing we can do about it, and besides, the Americans have brought it on themselves.'

'How?' asked Josef. His mother and father looked at each other.

'It's complicated, sweetheart,' said his mother urging her husband to shut up with her eyes.

They finished their dinner in an awkward silence, then later, after Anna had gone home and Josef was playing on the computer in his bedroom, his father knocked on his door, 'Can I come in?'

'Yeah,' Josef answered, without taking his eyes off the game. His father came in and sat down on bed. 'Listen, I want to talk to you about what happened today, in America.' Josef turned around in his chair to face him,

'What about it, dad?'

'Well, I think your old enough to understand.'

'Understand what?'

'Why these things happen,' his father said. 'Your mother thinks you're still a baby and we should shield you from these things as long as we can.'

'Why?'

'Because she's your mother and she loves you. I, on the other hand think you're a very intelligent and mature young man, and if you're old enough to have a girlfriend then you're old enough to know about this.' His father had a slight grin on his face. Josef felt his cheeks go red – he didn't know what to say. 'A blind man could see what's going on with you and Anna,' his father continued. 'She's a lovely girl, Josef.'

'I know, dad.'

'Anyway, you wanted to know what happened today?'

'Yeah, why did they do it?' said Josef, glad to be talking about something else.

'Because of religion,' said his father.

'Islam?'

'No, a certain kind of Islam. Extreme Islam.' His father went on to explain that all religions can be interpreted differently and even twisted to suit the needs of the user. He explained that because of America's involvement in the Middle East, they had made enemies. Josef listened intently and found a new respect for his father and when they had finished talking and his father got up to leave, Josef stopped him. 'Dad?'

'Yes son?'

'Thanks.'

'It's all right, Josef. That's what I'm here for.'

'Do you like Anna?'

'I think she's a lovely girl,' his father said, smiling as he left the room.

For the next few days all anybody talked about was what had happened in New York. Josef's teachers even talked about it in class and the school held a special assembly for it.

Josef was in a maths lesson when it happened. He didn't feel well – suddenly he felt faint and light-headed. The teacher sent him to the school nurse who decided to send him home for the day. She called his mother who was the first on the list of people to contact if anything was wrong with him but got no answer, so she called his father, who said it was ok to send Josef home. As no one could pick him up the nurse reluctantly agreed to let Josef walk home.

As Josef walked home, he thought about Anna – her smile, her laugh, her smell. They had strong feelings for each other and had talked about taking their relationship further and having sex. Anna wasn't sure if she was ready and Josef didn't want to push her. He smiled at Anna's house as he walked past Anna's house. His eye was drawn by a brand new silver BMW on the street and he thought how good it looked. As he approached his house he saw his mother's car on the drive. She must have come back home between the school calling and him walking home.

Josef turned the door handle and found that it was locked. Why had she locked the door? He got out his key, opened the door and went inside. He dropped his bag in the hall. 'Mum?' he shouted. There was noise upstairs and he heard movement. Then his mother appeared at the top of the stairs, she looked flustered. 'Hello sweetheart, what are you doing home? Is everything all right?'

'I didn't feel well, so the school sent me home.' As he spoke, a man appeared behind his mother. There was silence as Josef waited for his mother to explain who he was.

'Josef, this is my friend James,' she said as both of them came down the stairs. 'He's a friend from when I used to work at the barracks. I was just showing him the house.'

Josef didn't take his eyes off the man as he walked down the stairs.

'Hello, Josef,' he said, holding out his hand. He spoke with a British accent. Josef didn't shake his hand. Instead he went into the living room and sat on the sofa. He heard his mother say goodbye and some other words in English that Josef didn't understand. He heard the door close and his mother came into the living room and sat down next to him. 'Are you OK?' she asked.

'I'm fine,' he said, not looking at her.

'James is a friend of mine – he's a soldier,' she said.

'Is he dad's friend as well?'

'No. No he isn't. And I'd prefer if your father didn't know he was here. I don't think he'd understand.'

Josef looked at his mother. He wanted to be mad. He wanted to hate her.

'Fine' he said.

'Promise? Promise me, sweetheart,' she pressed.

'I won't say anything to dad.'

'That's a good boy. Do you want anything?'

'No. I'm going to go upstairs and have a lie down. I don't feel well.'

Josef lay on his bed for most of the afternoon, thinking about things. His mother. His father. Anna. A million thoughts whirled round his mind. He thought about the people in New York and all the things his grandfather had taught him. He thought about religion – and when he had finished thinking he played on his computer until he heard his father come home.

He went downstairs and into the kitchen where his mother and father were talking.

'Hello son, how are you feeling?' said his father.

'A little better.'

'Good, glad to hear it. Oh, you've got to be kidding me!' His father's attention had turned to the kitchen window. 'It's back, that cat! It's back.' He ran outside to shoo it off the lawn. Josef's mother laughed at the sight of his father chasing the cat out of their garden and Josef became angry. He stared at his mother and for the first time in a long time, he felt hatred. Josef's father came back into the kitchen. 'If I ever get hold of that cat, I'll kill it.'

'Don't be so dramatic – it's only a cat.'

'A cat that's ruining our lawn! What gives it the right to come on to our property and do whatever it wants?'

'It's a cat. It doesn't know any better,' said Josef's mother. 'Let it be.'

Josef listened to the conversation and he now knew what he must do – and for the next few days he thought about how he would do it. Every day after school he would watch for signs and after a while he found a pattern. He had to plan it carefully and do it when his parents were not at home.

One day about a week later, he pretended to be ill so his parents kept him off school. He stayed in bed until they both left the house and when he was sure they were gone he started his preparations.

He got his grandfather's knife out of his drawer, along with the wire trap he had made, just as the old man had taught him. The old Nazi had been useful for something after all these years. He went downstairs to the kitchen and got some meat out of the fridge, then he went out to the back garden to get everything ready.

He set the trap with the meat, then all he had to do was wait. He took cover behind a tree and wondered how long he would have to wait. Before long he saw the cat jump off the fence and into his garden. It looked around then caught the scent of the meat. It walked over to the meat and as it sniffed, Josef pulled the wire and the animal was caught. The wire tightened round its neck and it began to struggle. Josef got the knife from his pocket and ran over to the trap where the cat was hissing, yowling and struggling to break free. Josef griped the knife and in one smooth motion plunged into the animal's chest. It howled in pain and Josef thrust the knife in again and again. He held the body as the life drained out of it and watched its eyes fade into nothingness. There was blood everywhere – on his hands, his clothes and the grass. He stared at the limp body. What had he done? He'd killed a cat – an animal. He dropped the body in horror and looked at his bloody hands in disbelief. Josef started to cry as he gathered it up and carried it to the bin and put it in, along with the trap.

He picked up the bloody knife and went inside to clean himself up. He washed his hands, took his blood-stained clothes off and put them in the bin – a fitting shroud for the dead animal. He stayed in his bedroom until he heard a knock at the door. He checked the time – it must be

Anna come to see him. He went downstairs and answered the door, and there she was, more beautiful than ever. 'Are you ok?' she asked, looking at him.

'Not really.'

'What's the matter?'

'I just, I, I, don't feel right, that's all.' She placed her hand on the side of his face.

'You're a fucked-up character, Josef Reiniger' she said smiling at him. 'But that's why I like you. Come on, I've got something for you.' She took his hand and led him upstairs to his bedroom.

As they sat on the bed, Anna opened her bag and got out a pack of condoms. 'I think I'm ready, Josef,' she said holding his hand.

'OK.' He was not really sure what to do or say.

'Do you still want to?'

'Of course, it's just... I wasn't really expecting it to happen today.'

'Why? If we're both ready and want to do it, why not?'

Anna got off the bed and stood in front of him. She started to take off her clothes. She took off her shirt revealing her bra. Next she slowly removed her skirt. Then she took off her bra and stood before him in her knickers. She let him look at her body for a moment before she peeled off the last garment. She stood, naked, in front of him. He'd never seen anything so beautiful. She walked over close enough to touch.

'Your turn.' Josef took his clothes off and they stood in front of each other naked. He reached out to hold her and they kissed. He felt her naked body, her soft skin against his own. They got into his bed and they lost their virginity. It was amazing; Josef had never felt such pleasure, the joy of making love. He knew then, when he was inside her that he would love her for ever.

Josef would never forget that day – the day he lost more than his virginity. It was the day he lost his innocence. He never told anyone about what else he did that day – he didn't know how. The things his grandfather told him made more sense – the taking of life did change you and once you crossed that line there was no going back. For every life you took, you lost a little part of your soul – that was what the old man used to say. Josef never understood until now.

But he had Anna – she made him happy and their relationship grew stronger as time went by. Just as he no longer counted the many times they slept together, he lost count of the times his mother went to see the young British soldier – and how many time his father didn't notice because he was too caught up in his work.

Josef's life went on in the same way for what felt like a long time. He went to school, he spent time with Anna and he grew physically and mentally. He still didn't understand the world around him, as much as he tried. He followed the war on terror and current affairs with great interest, and did all the things a teenager does until one day, over three years after the day he lost his virginity and his innocence, Josef Reiniger's world came crashing down.

* * *

It was just after his sixteenth birthday when it happened. She told him to meet her at the takeaway after school. Josef and Anna now attended different schools – it was the German way, but missed seeing her every day. Now that they were older, they spent a lot of time in the city with their friends – her friends mostly. They would meet and hang out at the takeaway that was run by immigrants. They did pizzas, kebabs and all manner of junk food and they had an ample seating area, perfect for groups of teenagers. Josef didn't really like it, and only went because of her.

He left school and took the train into the city and headed for the takeaway, which had only just opened when he arrived. He sat down at a table and waited, playing with his mobile phone – looking like he had a life.

'Hello, Joe,' he heard someone say. Josef looked up and saw Kareem, the son, nephew or cousin of the owners – he was never sure.

'Do you need anything?' Kareem asked.

'No, I'm fine, thank you,' said Josef without looking up.

'OK, you let me know if you do.' Kareem went back behind the counter.

Josef checked the time – she was late. He hated waiting – it annoyed him that she could never be anywhere on time. To her, ten past the hour meant half past. It wasn't hard to be somewhere on time.

A few minutes later he heard the door open. He turned his head and there she was. Anna joined him. 'Hi Josef,' she said without kissing him, or even giving him a hug.

'Hello. Good day?'

'Fine' Neither of them said anything more. They just sat. He hated when she was like this.

'Do you want anything?' he asked.

'I'll have a Coke, please,' Josef went to the counter and Kareem bounded over to serve him. 'Yes Joe, what would you like?'

'Two Cokes, please'

'Two Cokes coming up. Glasses?'

'Please.' Kareem took two cans from the fridge. 'Ice?'

'Yes, please'

'Okey dokey. That's three euros please, Joe.'
Josef gave him the money, poured the Coke into
the glasses, and crushed the empty cans slightly
before pushing them back across the counter.

Josef sat down and gave Anna her glass.
'Thank you.' Her voice seemed strained.

'What's wrong?'

'Nothing.'

'Doesn't feel like nothing.'

Anna stared out of the window for few
moments then, without looking at him, said,
'It's over Josef. I want to split up.'

'What?'

'It's over. I think we should move on.' She
turned to look at him. Tears were beginning to
form in her eyes. 'I do love you Josef, a part of
me always will. But we've grown apart.'

'No we haven't.'

'We have Josef, since, I don't when – but
you're so distant all the time… and, and… sad.
You never smile or laugh any more.'

'What, so we just end it?'

'I think it's best.'

'But I love you.'

'I know you do Josef, and that's why this is so
hard. There's something I need to tell you.'

'What?'

'Last week, I went to a party – the one you
didn't want to go to.'

'Yes, and?' he pursued.

'Well, I…'

'Anna, you can tell me anything.'

'I slept with someone else.'

Josef stared out of the window, then down at the table. He looked around the takeaway, at the counter, at the ovens in the back, at the other tables and at the menu on the wall.

'You did?' Josef still couldn't look her in the face.

'Josef, I'm sorry. It was a mistake – a stupid drunken mistake. But I did it. We haven't been right for a while and if things were OK then I wouldn't have done it, would I? So I think it's time we split up and moved on with our lives.'

For while Josef didn't say anything. He stared at the table.

'Say something Josef, please.'

'Who was it?'

'Does it matter?'

'Yes.' He finally lifted his head to look at her.

'He's just a guy that goes to the school near mine.'

'Do you love him?'

'What? No, of course not. It was a mistake.'

'Fine. If this is what you want. Go. Let's split up. You can do whatever you want then, can't you? You can drop your knickers for everyone.'

'Josef, I…'

'Go, go on – and leave me alone. I won't stop you.'

'I'm sorry Josef. I hope you can forgive me one day and we can be friends.'

'FUCK OFF! I NEVER WANT TO SEE YOU AGAIN!'

Anna began to cry, then she got up and left Josef alone.

He felt tears pricking his eyes and his throat tightening. He grabbed some napkins from the dispenser and wiped his eyes, then sat staring out of the window as the world went on about its business – passing cars, pedestrians, cyclists.

'Here you go, Joe,' He looked up, and Kareem was holding a paper plate with a slice of pepperoni pizza – Josef's favourite. Kareem put it on the table 'On the house, my friend' he said. Josef didn't know what to say other than 'Thank you.'

'Mind if I sit?' Kareem asked.

'Feel free,' Josef replied, grateful for the company.

'Women! Complete bitches!' said Kareem, trying to hide the awkwardness of the situation.

'Yeah,' Josef agreed. 'You heard all that?'

'Yes, my friend. And I'm sorry your heart is broken.'

'Thanks.'

'But it will mend. It always does.'

'Yeah, maybe.'

'And we may not be as pretty as she is, but you're always welcome here.' Kareem smiled as he got up and left Josef alone.

Josef finished the pizza, said goodbye to Kareem and went out on to the street. How could she do this? He crossed a road leading to a plaza with a fountain and monuments and he sat down on a bench. She was supposed to love me? Why? Why? Am I not good enough? Why didn't she talk to me? I love her. I loved her. Fuck her. The bitch. Let her rot. I want to see her, touch her, and feel her. Her taste. Her smell. Why has this happened? Was she right? If that's what she wants fine. Fuck her. The whore. He had his dick inside her. Was he handsome? Was he bigger? His hands were on her body. His lips on her lips. There naked bodies. Fuck her. I hate her. I hope she suffers. Fucking bitch.

'Excuse me, do you have a light?' Josef looked up and saw a woman standing with an unlit cigarette. She was dressed for a night out, short skirt, revealing top, make-up overdone and a lot of perfume.

'No, sorry.'

The woman put the cigarette away. 'Bad habit, anyway. You look lost. Are you all right?' she asked with a sympathetic smile.

Josef looked at her, she was older than he was
– a real woman. 'I'm OK.'

You don't look OK. Mind if I join you?' He
nodded to her to sit down.

As she sat down, her skirt rode up revealing
most of her legs. He tried not look at them, or
her ample cleavage. He could smell her perfume
– it was quite heady.

'What's your name, sweetheart?' she said.

'Josef.'

'That's a nice name. I'm Ricci. I knew a Josef
once – nice guy. Are you a nice guy, Josef?' she
said and placed her hand on his thigh.

'I try to be.'

'With me you can be anything you want to
be.' She began to run her fingers through the
hair on the back of his head. It felt nice, and he
wanted to kiss her and hold her body and make
love to this woman.

'I have a place not far from here. It's 50 euros
for half an hour, or 80 for a full hour.'

'Is it?' Josef said, as the penny dropped. He
gazed at her bare legs and ran his eyes up to her
cleavage.

'OK,' he said, 'but first I need a bank,
though.'

'There's one on the way. Lets go.' She stood
up to leave and Josef went with her. They walked
side by side to a bank machine where he drew

out 100 euros from the account his father made sure was always stocked for him.

'This way.' She led him to an apartment building that looked like it was purpose built for this kind of thing. It was rough – the kind of place where they find dead bodies in the movies.

They walked through the doors and up a flight of stairs, down a corridor and round a corner, and Ricci stopped at a door with a brass number five on it. Once inside, she switched on a light, revealing a room that was more like a hotel than an apartment. There was a double bed with only an under sheet and on the bedside table were some condoms and lotions as well as a box of latex gloves. She took off her coat and put it on the chair in the corner of the room. Closing the door, she held out her hand to Josef. 'How long?'

'Half an hour,' he replied and, taking out his wallet, gave her 50 euros. She smiled at him, took the money and put it in her bag before she turning to put her arms over his shoulders. She lent in and kissed him, putting her tongue in his mouth. Josef was surprised – he didn't think they kissed on the mouth. He kissed her back – this was different, colder. She rotated her tongue round his, he lifted her short skirt and let his hands wander.

'Get undressed,' she ordered. Josef complied while she peeled off her skirt and top, followed by her underwear. 'Get on the bed and lie back.' He lay on the bed and watched as she crept up to him like a cat, stopping at his waist. She inspected the area round his groin and began to gently stroke him, and as he went hard, she rubbed her breasts around it. She leaned over him so her breasts were hovering above his face; he kissed them and sucked them as she got out a condom. She put it on him with her mouth and began to suck. It felt amazing – but a lot different to the way Anna did it. She stopped and grabbed a bottle of lotion; she rubbed some of it between her legs and then guided him inside her. She rocked backwards and forwards on top him. His hands explored her body. But he didn't want to do it like this. He moved her round and got on top of her, she spread her legs wide as he relieved the pain and anger he was feeling in his heart. He went faster and faster, then moved her hands above her head and held them down. He went harder and harder, making her moan. He heard his mobile phone ringing from his jeans pocket on the floor, but he ignored it as his body moved forwards and backwards, again and again until he exploded inside her and rested on top of her.

He withdrew and lay down next to her. 'Did you enjoy that?' she asked, running her fingers across his face. Josef nodded as she got up and cleaned herself up. She threw some baby-wipes on the bed, he removed the condom and wiped himself, wrapping up the condom in a baby-wipe. He felt awkward and guilty – this was wrong somehow.

They got dressed in silence then she gave him a hug and a kiss before showing him out. The door closed behind him and he walked down the corridor alone. He left the building and headed through the busy streets toward the station. Waiting to cross a road, he checked his phone – a missed call, voicemail and a text, all from Anna. He ignored all of them and put his phone away. Josef stared out of the window as the train sped him away. He felt guilty, dirty, sordid. He wanted a shower, to scrub himself clean. He thought about ringing Anna back. Fuck her.

It was late as he walked back to his house along the deserted suburban streets, he noticed that his clothes smelled of the whore's perfume – or was it his skin? Whatever it was, he was repulsed by it.

He rounded the corner of his street and felt a pain and longing in his heart as he walked past Anna's house. He stopped at the end of her front garden for a moment, then carried on to his house.

As usual, his parents were not home. His father would be at the office with his secretary and his mother with her soldier.

He took a carton of orange juice from the fridge and drank straight from the carton, spilling it down his chin. He walked through the cold empty house to his bedroom, undressed and sat naked on his bed for a few minutes before going for a shower. The steam from the shower filled the bathroom, the heat from it felt nice against his skin. He got into the shower and began to scrub himself, removing the dirt and filth from every inch of body the way a surgeon would before an operation. He scrubbed and scrubbed until his skin was raw, went back to his room to get dry.

He put on clean shorts and a t-shirt and, as he closed his wardrobe door, he saw himself in the mirror. He gazed upon his own face, taking in every detail. He rested his head against his reflection. Josef gently tapped his head against it – then did it again, only harder, and again harder still. He head-butted his reflection hard enough to hurt a few times before roaring at himself. Standing back, he threw a fist at himself, again and again – and he didn't stop until the glass had shattered, his fist was covered in blood and his eyes were filled with tears.

Josef tried to compose himself. He used the still-damp towel to clean his hand, carefully removing the little shards of glass and the pain started to hit him. He lay on the bed, nursing his hand, and thought about what had happened to him today. When he got up that morning the world was fine. He'd had breakfast and gone to school. When he got up that morning he had a loving girlfriend and was happy. Then she dumped him – she had cheated on him. She had had sex with someone else… and so had he.

Everything was different now. He didn't have a girlfriend any more. Who was she with? Was she having sex, right now, with someone else? He looked around his room trying to find something different, but it was just the way he left it that morning. It was the same.

He scanned through the photos on his mobile phone and stopped at one of him with Anna – both smiling and happy. He had ignored it before, but now he dialled his voicemail and listened to her message. 'Josef it's me. I'm so sorry. I didn't want it to end like this. Please ring me back.'

Josef deleted the message, then proceeded to delete all the texts she had sent him. In his 'contacts' he scrolled to Anna. Options… a message appeared 'Delete Anna?' The options offered were 'Yes' and 'no'. He paused for a moment then pressed 'Yes', and she was gone. Josef got into bed, turned off the light and went to sleep.

Over the next few days Josef skulked around the house. On the brief occasion that he saw his parents, he told them that he wasn't well and had a cold. He stayed off school and stayed in his room for hours on end, playing computer games, watching films, listened to music and surfing the internet, illegally downloading music and films.

They called it 'peer-to-peer file-sharing' and it was illegal, but everyone did it nonetheless. It provided free music and films as well as TV shows from America, computer games and even books. Who wouldn't do it, and who did it harm? The artists and filmmakers? Josef downloaded a film that had made over a billion US dollars at the box office. The actors, director, and producers had been paid millions, and the studio that made it, itself a subsidiary of a huge multinational corporation, made a profit of over 800 million dollars. And yet the film industry was filled with righteous indignation when people downloaded their films for free instead of paying 15 euros for a dvd. They said it damaged the industry and stifled creativity. Was 800 million dollars not enough? Greed really does know no bounds.

Musicians and singers were the same. Josef read an interview with the lead singer of a very well known rock band who was complaining that people downloaded his music illegally. It was wrong, he said – it was stealing and it should be stopped. This man was worth over 100 million dollars and he was telling people who would never, ever have anywhere near that amount of money the difference between right and wrong. This was the same man who, in his native country, had been caught avoiding the highest rate of tax by using clever loopholes. Hypocrisy, too, knows no bounds.

It was the same story that had been played out for centuries. The haves and the have nots – the rich, famous and powerful, and everybody else. The elite did what they pleased and got away with it because they had money and connections. Politicians, media magnates, so-called celebrities, actors, sportsman – and the multinational corporations that owned all their souls – treated the masses like mindless sheep. And these 'sheeple' did nothing about it. They swallowed it all – and for reasons beyond understanding, asked the elite for still more and more.

One of the more ludicrous things the sheeple fell for was the invitation to register their comments on websites, blogs and on-line news articles. Capitalism truly proved itself to be the perfect system. The elite and big business had found a way to reach out and show the sheeple 'we care' and 'we value your opinion' – 'we want to know what you think' – the subtext being, 'we've given you all our usual bullshit but have found a way to make you accept it, imagining you have free will. You can say whatever you want (in a time and place of our choosing), which will make you feel that you're part of the conversation, part of the debate, part of the world – then you'll be content and carry on doing nothing while we continue to step all over you.'

Josef thought about some of the news articles he read and the inevitable comments that they provoked. It was a stroke of genius. Anyone could comment on everything and anything – and do it anonymously. If there was online news story about a new government policy, the ensuing comments made for fun reading. Josef never knew that were so many experts and statesmen amongst the general public, who could clearly do a much better job of running the country than those currently doing it. They had all the answers – it was so easy.

It didn't matter what the article was about – politics, entertainment, sports – the experts gathered to comment on each one, and told the world their opinion, and woe betide anyone who disagreed with them. They were clearly in the right, so how dare anyone hold a different opinion from theirs? These 'experts' then turned on each other, posting vile comments and insults. It was pathetic.

Josef wondered if they really believed anyone cared what they thought. Who were these people who commented on articles online? No-one wants, needs or cares about what you think about anything. Who are you? Are you something special? Do you have unique skills and talents – or are you just a sad, pathetic loser – an insignificant blotch on life. A failure who feels the need to post their thoughts on the internet because your life is so meaningless. If you were so special and your thoughts and opinions mattered, people would be writing articles about you, wouldn't they? But they're not. You vent your anger, bitterness and hatred on the world in the safest way possible, without risk of facing any consequences. But that's just the way they want you – safe in line, like all the others. So you never stop to think what's happening to your world. Who is worse, the fool, or the fool who follows? People are strange – they bitch and moan about the world, about the corrupt and useless politicians, and yet they can't be bothered to anything about it. It struck

Josef that the Christian God had vanished long
ago and democracy had been rotting in its grave
a long time – and all the while the illusion of
freedom cast its shadow on the western world,
hiding the true nature of free market capitalism.

After hours on-line, absorbed by his
thoughts, Josef turned off his computer and
looked round his bedroom. Is this it? Is this what
life is? Was there nothing more? A job, a family,
money. He needed to get out of the house – get
some air. He got dressed, went out and caught
the train into the city.

Josef decided he'd go to the takeaway – it
would be open by the time he arrived and maybe
Anna and her friends would be there.

In the city he watched all the people scurrying
about their business and thought how shallow
and empty it all was. When he arrived at the
takeaway no-one was there, so he went over
to the counter and saw Kareem who smiled
warmly at him. 'Josef! Good to see you, my
friend. You've not been around.'

'I know, been a bit busy.'

'What can I get you – anything you want, on
the house.'

'Are you sure? I can pay.'

'Friends don't pay,' Kareem said with a grin.
Josef thought about the concept and smiled. 'All
right. Just a Coke please'

Kareem smiled as he gave him the drink. 'So, what you been up to, Joe?'

'Nothing much.'

'Thinking about your woman?' Kareem asked. Josef looked at him.

'A little bit. Has she been in?'

Kareem nodded. 'She was in the other night with some friends.'

'Girls or boys?'

'Both.'

'Right.' Josef took a drink.

'You know what we do to adulterers in our country?' Kareem said.

'What?'

'We stone them to death. In countries where my religion is adhered to, adultery is not tolerated.'

'You're a Muslim?' Josef asked.

'I am, and proud of it. It gives meaning and purpose to life.'

'That must be nice.'

'It is. Are you religious Joe?'

Josef laughed. 'No, not at all. No offence, but I don't believe a word of any of it.'

'Any of what?'

'Religion, faith – any of it.'

'All religion, or just Christianity?'

'I don't know. I've never really thought about it like that.'

'Maybe you should.'

'Mmmm… So where are you from originally?'

'My family moved here from Turkey when I was small.'

'How do you like Germany?'

'It's nice… but the weather…' he said rubbing his shoulders.

Josef and his new friend talked some more, finding out about each other and their lives and interests until customers came in and Kareem had to work. Josef took a seat at a table and played with his phone until Kareem joined him on his break, bringing Josef a pizza, which he ate while they talked about everything and anything – girls, football, music and films, religion and politics.

Josef felt a connection to Kareem, as if they were cut from the same cloth, and even though they were from different countries, and cultures they bonded very quickly. When Kareem had to go back work, Josef picked up a newspaper that had been left by another customer. It was filled with nothing but bad news – page after page of the darker side of humanity. Crime, scandal, corruption. It made for very depressing reading, even the stories about famous people. Why did anybody care what a pop star snorted up their nose or where a footballer put their dick?

An outcry and self-righteous hypocrisy from the journalists and columnists at the scandal. Really? A rich and famous young man cheats on his wife with a model. Are we that surprised? Are we really that shocked and appalled? And do we really care?

Josef closed the paper and got out his phone to play a game, so he didn't notice the group come in or see who they were – he only heard the door open and voices talking loudly. He took no notice of them until the shouting started.

'There's a hair in my burger!' a loud voice announced. Josef looked up and saw a group of young men at the counter. A couple of them were wearing Jewish skullcaps.

'So sorry, my friend. I'll get you another,' Kareem offered.

'I'm not your friend,' said the young man with the burger. Josef didn't like his tone and put his phone away to watch what was going on.

'Hey, Abdul, get me a Coke while you're there,' said another of the boys. Josef could tell they were drunk or high by the way they talked and stood. Kareem came back with another burger for the young man and gave it to him, but he didn't even say thank you.

'Where's my Coke?' the other boy demanded, and Kareem hurried to get him one.

'Fucking useless Arab,' said one of them, and they all laughed.

Josef got up from the table and walked over to the young men, still at the counter. 'Apologise.'

'What? Who the fuck are you?' one of them challenged.

'I'm nobody, friend. But apologise to him.' Josef said and pointed at Kareem.

'It's OK, Joe. Leave it,' said Kareem shaking his head.

'Yes, Joe. Leave it,' said another, mocking Kareem's accent. The boy with the burger walked up to Josef and pushed his head up against his. 'Fuck off, right now,' he said.

'Or what?' said Josef, pushing back.

'Or we'll crush your fucking skull, then piss on you' said the young man.

'I'll bet you a can of Zyclon B you won't, you Jew cunt,' said Josef with a wide grin. The young man threw down his burger and pushed Josef, who went flying back. Josef got ready to swing but someone held him back.

'Don't, Joe. Their time will come.' It was Kareem who had come from behind the counter to put a stop to the brawl. Before the young men could do anything there was a loud crash behind them. They all turned to look – one of Kareem's brothers had smashed a baseball bat down on the counter. He told the young Jewish men to leave – which, reluctantly, they did, all looking daggers at Josef. Kareem let Josef go. 'Why did you do that, Josef? It was fine. We're use to things like that.'

'It's wrong,' said Josef. 'There's no need for it.'

'They were drunk and, like I said, their time will come,' said Kareem calmly. Josef looked him in the eye and somehow knew what he meant.

'Yeah, OK.' Josef relented.

Josef sat down and Kareem brought him another drink, and sat with him as they talked some more. Josef stayed until well after the takeaway closed and Kareem introduced him to his brothers and cousins. They sat and talked into the early hours, telling Josef about Islam and what it meant to live your life as a Muslim. They explained to him the daily prayers, the rituals and festivals of Islam and Josef drank it all in, asking questions and telling them about his life, his parents, his school, his ex-girlfriend, his taste in music, his hobbies and what he thought about politics.

Josef checked the time; the last train home would be leaving soon. He said goodbye to his new friends with much hand-shaking and hugging and caught the train. At home, for once mother and father were both in, but they were asleep, his mother in their bedroom and his father on the sofa in his study.

Sometimes he wished they would just divorce and get it over with. Neither of them was happy – and hadn't been for a long time. Why did they carry on the facade? Why pretend to be a married couple when you were anything but? If you don't love someone and don't want to be with them, just say so. Why go out and cheat and have affairs? Just tell the person you don't love them any more, for whatever reason, and end it instead of hurting them more. Josef knew his parents hurt every time they saw each other. They both knew about the other's transgressions but both were too stupid or too scared to let go. It was a sham – the elephant in the room no-one talked about.

Josef went up to his bedroom and tried to sleep, but his thoughts kept him awake for hours. Why didn't they just divorce? Was it for his sake? He felt they'd all be better off if they went their separate ways. He didn't care. Thoughts raced through his head, prompted by what he had learned that evening. If we were in a Muslim country this wouldn't happen. They'd be stoned to death. Good. Fuck them. Liars. We could do Anna as well, the little whore. Beautiful eyes. Fuck her. Why am I always lonely? Nobody likes me. No-one understands me. I miss the old man. I could talk to him. He never judged, and he didn't ignore me. He respected me. But then he left me alone, the old bastard. Those Jew cunts – how dare they? Bouncing around like they own the world – being vile to Kareem. I like Kareem. He's nice. He understands. I had a good time tonight. Islam's really interesting. Never knew it was like that. I'll buy some books on it. Maybe I'll get a copy of the Qur'an. I can ask Kareem. He'd help me learn more about it.

Josef was wide awake. He got out of bed and turned on his computer and started to surf the Internet. His sixteen-year-old body felt an urge, and he went on to an adult website and masturbated while watching a video. Satisfied, he went back to his homepage and read an article about a new law that had been proposed in the *Bundestag*. Politics was a joke. A man of the people, elected by the people, to speak for the people he hadn't seen for decades. In reality it was a man of the party, chosen by the party, to implement the policies of the party. The people were nothing more than a commodity to be stripped down to numbers, statistics and demographics. 'If we say this, white men in their thirties will vote for us. If we say we will do this, we'll get young people's support, and if we say this, we'll get the housewives.'

Josef thought politics was a very unsavoury world. Instead of applying logic, reason and fairness and doing things that would benefit the majority of people and ensure a safe, prosperous and secure society, they wallowed in ideology, dogma and party politics and worshipped at the alter of power. Because in the end, that's all it was. It wasn't about the politics or the people – it was about the power.

Josef had read somewhere that people who want to be politicians should be barred from ever becoming one. All this just reinforced to Josef how messed up the world was. What was the point? None of it made any sense. Grow up, go to school, get an education. When you've finished with education, get a job. Get a wife. Get some children. Buy a house. Fill up the house with things. Buy a car. Go on holidays once or twice a year. Eat out.

Watch films and television, read books. Play sports. Get a hobby. Work for forty years and then retire. Then simply wait for death. Is this all there was?

Was this freedom? Was all this fulfilling… or was it all meaningless? Were we all just sitting on a rock travelling round a star at unfathomable speed, just waiting for the ride to be over? Nothing lasts forever; even the stars burn out and fade into nothingness.

Josef turned the computer off and got back into bed. He lay awake with no hope of sleeping. Why was he so empty? So lonely? Why did life hold no appeal for him? Surely there had to be more. There had to be meaning somewhere – anywhere. Something that gave order, structure and meaning to life. Was there a higher power at work? Some mysterious force or being responsible for creation and life?

The Christian God had never convinced Josef, and religion had never played a big part of his life. There had to be more. Did what Kareem and his family believe make sense? He didn't know – but he was curious. He would learn more about it. There had to be something that made sense of it all.

* * *

Over the following weeks and months Josef spent more and more time at Kareem's takeaway. He bought a translated copy of the Qur'an and spent hours talking with Kareem and his family about the sacred text.

His home life became non-existent as his parents grew further and further apart, until one day he got home from school and found the rare sight of both their cars on the drive. He walked into the living room where he found the ominous sight of both his parents waiting for him.

'What's going on?'

They both looked at him as if he was eight. 'Sit down, Josef, there's something we need to talk about,' said his mother. He looked at his father who signalled that it was OK. Josef sat down on the sofa opposite them.

'Josef, there's no easy way to say this,' his father began.

'You're getting a divorce?' Josef asked. His parents looked at each other then at him.

'Yes sweetheart, we are, but we…'

'You want me to know you both love me very much and it's not my fault, and all that other rubbish,' said Josef bluntly.

'Josef! Don't speak to your mother like that.'

'Really? Or what?'

'I'm leaving, Josef,' said his mother. 'Things haven't been right between your father and me for a while now and…'

'Save it, woman!' said Josef. 'I hope you both know that adultery is considered a sin, and you'll both burn for it.'

An uneasy silence fell across the room. His father got up and as he walked out, he turned. 'When you have calmed down, Josef, I'm here if you want to talk like men, not little boys.' And he walked out. His mother sat down next to Josef on the couch. 'Oh sweetheart, I'm sorry. But this is for the best.'

'Yes, yes it is,' he agreed.

'And you know I'm only a phone call away. You'll have to come and visit.'

'Enjoy your life, mother,' Josef said coldly as he got up from the couch and walked out of the room. Behind him he could hear her start to sob.

He went to his bedroom and slammed the door behind him. He lay on his bed and festered until he heard a car pull up outside. He got up to look – it was a taxi. He watched as his mother walked out with her suitcases, got in and was driven away. Good riddance, whore, he thought as he turned on the computer.

He logged into his Facebook account and scrolled through his newsfeed. Social networking? There was nothing social about it. Facebook, twitter and all the other websites that were meant to keep people connected did nothing but separate them. Millions of stupid people, interacting virtually with millions of other stupid people. It was pathetic. Like, comment, tweet, re tweet, message. Why? Why had this become an accepted part of life? To bring people closer together? Tell that to the girl who slit her wrists after she read the vile comments on her Facebook page, or the other countless victims of abuse. Friends and followers? It was a joke. Josef didn't care about other people's children or how well they did at school. He didn't care about the jokes, photos of animals, political comments and inspirational quotes people posted. He only went on to sneer at the sheeple. Is this what life will be – lived online? The last bastion of freedom and liberty had been wiped away, with the right to privacy willingly handed over. It was just another means of control.

To Josef the tragedy was that freedom had not been lost to tyranny or oppression. No-one wanted to round people up. The real tragedy lay in the fact that millions of people had given up their freedoms for nothing more than profit. As soon as you 'like' something on Facebook, within minutes adverts will appear on your page related to what you 'like', as if by magic. They know who you are, what you look like, who your friends are. They know what you do for living, what religion you follow, what political party you support, how many children you have and who your relatives are. They know what music, films, TV, books, hobbies and sports you like. Around the globe, millions of people had willingly composed their own personal profile – but it was safe. It's only Facebook or twitter or whatever. But what goes on the internet stays on the internet – for ever.

Governments spend millions every ten years or so, compiling data about their citizens from a census. In the future they won't need to – they'll just ask Facebook.

Josef had a notification – it was an invitation to a party at a nightclub in the city, from Anna. He clicked it and found out where it was and what time. Then he clicked on her name and was taken to her profile page. He looked at her status updates then went to her photos, clicking on the album that said 'holiday' and browsed her photos. She looked good in a bikini. He stared at the photo of her semi-naked body and masturbated as he thought about her.

He clicked back on to the event page. Should he go? It had been months since he had last seen her, but yet she had invited him. He shut down the computer and contemplated going to the party. Why had she invited him? Did she actually want to see him? Or had she just invited everyone on her 'friends' list?

Josef made up his mind – he would go, and searched through his wardrobe for something to wear. Suitably attired, he set out for club. There was Anna. She was still beautiful – but she was different. She had moved on with her life without him. She was happy. He had thought he would want to get back with her when he saw her face again, but to his amazement he didn't. When he looked at her he felt nothing – they had a polite conversation above the music. She was beautiful, yes – but that was no longer enough for Josef. Sex was sex. He wanted and needed more.

He made his excuses and got out the heat, smoke and noise of the nightclub. The club scene had never appealed to him – he didn't get what all the fuss was about. You pay to go into a place where you have to shout to talk to anyone, where you pay over the odds for sub-standard drinks and spend your evening squashed like a sardine, scarcely able to move. There was a reason people took drugs before going in; you had to be high to enjoy it. And it was nothing new – for thousands of years people had gathered and danced around a fire to the beat of the drums. Was this any different?

Out on the street, the cool night air was a welcome relief after the claustrophobic confines of the club. He made his way to Kareem's takeaway – he craved intelligent conversation with people who accepted and understood him. As he walked, Josef looked around the streets and felt nothing but contempt. Had he changed? Or was it the world that had changed? Or had his eyes simply been opened to the world?

At the takeaway Josef was met with greetings from Kareem and his brothers. He took his usual seat where Kareem brought him a Coke and sat down with him.

'How are you, my friend?'

'I'm good,' said Josef. He took a drink of Coke and looked Kareem straight in the eye. 'I've been thinking.'

'Oh, what about?'

Josef paused. 'I want to become a Muslim,' he said.

Kareem smiled and stood up. Without warning he punched Josef hard in the mouth.

When Josef looked up, it wasn't Kareem that had hit him – it was Andy Baker. He was no longer in the takeaway. He wasn't even in Germany and his name was no longer Josef Reiniger. His name was Khalid and he was in the Four Freedoms Tower in London, on a sacred mission for Allah. He was trapped inside a lift with this infidel called Andy Baker. Andy had attacked him and now they were fighting – and Khalid was losing.

17

Inside the lift shaft, the steel cables holding up the lift quivered like the strings on a violin. Another two strands came loose.

Inside the concrete staircase that made up the core of the building, Inspector Taylor and the young policeman ran breathlessly to the door marked 50. The inspector doubled over trying to catch his breath.

'Jesus Christ. Oooh. Bloody hell, this was a bad idea.'

'I hear that, sir.'

'Right, come on then.' They went through the fire door and entered the corridor and checked along the identical doors for the right number.

'Here we go sir, this is the one.'

The inspector joined the constable at the door and knocked. Nothing. He knocked again. No answer.

'Well, he's either still in bed or not in.' The inspector contemplated the door for a moment.

'Kick it in, constable.'

'Are you sure, sir? We don't have a warrant or anything.'

'Don't worry. If I'm wrong – and I hope to God I am – I'll take it on the chin.'

'OK, sir. Stand back.' The young policeman kicked the door as hard as he could. Nothing. The door didn't budge. He made another attempt. Then another.

On the third attempt, the door flew open, sending splinters into the air.

'OK son, you wait here. Give me your torch.'

The inspector went inside and walked down the hall. He came to a half-open door and gently pushed it open. Bathroom. He found the living room and walked in. Switching on the lights, he noticed how well-appointed it was – the décor and the furniture. It would've been nice, apart from the smell and the mess. Stale tobacco and body odour. He glanced round the room –whoever lived here was a scruffy bastard, he thought. Dirty washing on the floor, days' worth of dirty pots in the sink, and empty take away boxes in stacks.

As he looked round the room, his eye fell on a well-used copy of *The Qur'an*. He flicked through the pages and saw that certain passages were marked. He put the book down, then and out of the corner of his eye he saw it, on the kitchen table. He went over and knew immediately. It was him. On the table were empty bottles of powered bleech, remnants of fibre glass and empty packets of nails bought from a well known chain of DIY stores. This was the guy.

He turned away from the remnants of bomb-making and saw in the corner of the room; box upon box of empty and discarded fireworks, available from most supermarkets near bonfire night. He had emptyied them all of their gunpowder. So simple, so easy, yet so terrifying. An image of a packed tube car flashed through John's mind. He made eye contact with the cartoon Guy Fawkes on the side of one of the boxes. The irony wasn't lost on the inspector, if it wasn't so tragic it would be funny. A man celebrated every year in the UK for trying to blow up parliament nearly 400 years ago – providing the means for a modern terrorist to kill and maim hundreds. The inspector turned and ran out of the apartment.

The young PC was waiting anxiously outside. 'COME ON – IT'S HIM,' he yelled. The young policeman followed him as they ran back down the stairs.

'Are you sure, sir?'

'YES! I'm sure. Come on, we need to get that lift to the ground.'

As they rushed back down the winding concrete stairwell, the inspector didn't even notice his breathlessness – he only thought of success. The guy was stuck in the lift – they had him! This would be an easy catch.

When they reached the ground floor they burst through the doors into reception. 'Right, guys, it's him. The guy in the lift – that's our man.'

The other police officers glanced at each other. The concierge looked as if he was going to be sick.

'We need to get armed response and bomb squad down here ASAP,' said the inspector. 'You, what's your name?' he turned to Bob.

'Bob, Bob Fitzpatrick.'

'Right, Bob, pretty soon this place is going to be crawling with people. You need to call your bosses. You have procedures in place for something like this, don't you?'

'Err, yes, yes we do.'

'OK then, you get going on what you need to do. When is this engineer going to be here?'

'Any minute now.'

'OK, good stuff. He smiled at Bob. 'We've got the bastard!'

18

Inside the lift, Andy and Khalid sat back in opposite corners – only this time Andy had the gun. He nursed a split lip as he pointed it at Khalid who had a broken nose. Silence.

Andy wiped away some of the blood from his lip. He looked at it for moment, then at Khalid.

'Your blood.'

'What of it?'

'It's the same colour as mine.'

Khalid looked bewildered.

'Maybe we're not so different after all?' said Andy.

'I… am… nothing like you. And I never will be. I hate everything you stand for, you fucking pig.' Khalid spat at the floor.

'Do you really? I think you're delusional. I think you're a very troubled and confused young man. I think you've latched on to something you don't fully understand and have used it as an excuse to vent your own hatred and bitterness.'

'You dare! You dare question my faith?'

'Faith? This isn't faith. This is madness.

Khalid stared at him.

'You've found a spine.'

'No, just a gun.'

'And what do you plan on doing with it?'

'I'm going to make sure you get arrested when we get out of here.'

'Really?'

'Yes.'

'Hmph.'

'So tell me, why are you here? Why are you doing this?'

'I've told you! I'm here to do god's work, kafir.'

'No, I meant what made you become a Muslim? And then take it to the extreme. I can't place your accent.'

'I was born in Germany.'

'Germany?'

'You want to know why a young westerner, from a rich, first-world nation would convert to Islam?'

'Yes,' said Andy. 'I don't understand. It's one thing if you're born into it and have lived with it your whole life – then you can have an understanding of it and maybe believe a different interpretation – but you? I just don't get it.'

Khalid smiled – not the smile of happiness, but the polite, smug, superior smile people use when they think they know something you don't. The smile of politicians when they talk to their constituents. The smile of journalists and media men when they interview ordinary people. A smile that says, 'I'm better than you. I know more than you.'

'Get it?' said Khalid. 'You don't see what's around you? Our countries are virtually the same. The whole of the west is nigh on identical. You don't see?'

'See what?'

'It's disgusting! Our whole stinking way of life! Our whole culture is a giant filthy mess!

Andy lowered the gun slightly.

'And that's why you converted? Because what? Our society has problems? You need some serious help.'

'Do I? Or is it the rest of the world that needs help? What do we live for? All we do is scurry about, trying to eke out a living, while a few privileged individuals lord it over the masses. The system itself is flawed. It's all geared around money – the getting and keeping of money and wealth. And what do those with money do? They make us think we need all this shit – all this garbage – computers, mobile phones, the internet. A nice house, with nice furniture. They make us believe we need these things – that we want these things. That somehow if you buy an expensive car your life will be better. Or if you wear a certain thing or use a certain product, somehow you will be more appealing to the opposite sex. It's nonsense. It's all about keeping the masses down and the few in control.'

Andy thought about what Khalid was saying.

'Wait' said Andy. 'What you're talking about isn't faith – it's got nothing to do with religion. It's about capitalism. You're talking about our financial system – which is worldwide. How is that anything to do with Islam, or any of it?'

'It has everything to do with it! The materialism of the West has murdered the Christian God – and our values, our ethics and our faith died with him. And Islam – Islam is the only true answer!'

'The answer to what?'

'Life!'

'What happened to you to make you this way? I know you weren't born with this hatred. You weren't born wanting to do this.'

'I was born into a world that has forgotten human decency. This world – our way of life – is an affront to god!'

'So it should be burned? So people deserve to die? Well here's something to think about. I was born into this world too, and so was everyone else. How can we be held responsible for things out of our control and that happened before any of us were even born?'

Silence returned once more – a stalemate. An unstoppable force had met an immovable object.

'You still haven't told me,' Andy pursued.

'What?'

'Why you would do this.'

'I have told you. It is god's will.'

Andy was getting frustrated; all he wanted was an answer, a reason for this madness.

'OK then, why Islam? Why not Hinduism, or Buddhism or any of the other religions? What happened to make you have THIS faith?'

'I woke up,' said Khalid. 'I realised that our way of life was wrong – it's all focused on material things and I wanted, I WANT more. I want meaning and purpose – and Islam is that purpose.'

Finally, Andy thought, he's beginning to open up.

'Is our world that bad, though? I mean, I'm the same as you, pretty much born in a western country. And I've never really had a problem with it. I like having nice things. I like my phone and everything it can do. I love the internet and all the other trappings of modern life. Does that make me a bad person? Do I deserve to die?'

'Yes!' Khalid replied, without blinking or hesitation. 'Ignorance is not bliss: It's sinful.'

Andy knew his cause was lost – he wasn't going to get through to him, but at least he still had the gun. At least now Khalid couldn't hurt anyone, but there was still a nagging thought at the back of Andy's mind. 'What about your family? Do they deserve to die too?'

'Humph. They more than most.'

'WHY?' said Andy, stunned.

'They represent everything I want to fight against – greed, adultery, sin!'

Of all the hate inside Khalid's soul, this revelation disturbed Andy more than anything else. He could understand a little the frustration of modern life – the injustice – but this… never. Family was sacred.

'What did they do to you to make you feel this way?'

'So you're going to try and psychoanalyse me now, doctor? HA!' Khalid spat. 'You're pathetic! You're so arrogant that if you meet someone who thinks differently, who doesn't tow the party line, who disagrees with conventional thinking, then there must be something wrong with them.' Khalid's smile returned. Andy's grip on the pistol tightened.

'I've never met anyone who thought murder, violence and hate were acceptable behaviour.'

'That's because you're wrapped up in cotton wool. You've never seen the real world. The West is so arrogant, so pretentious. Why? Because you have this blanket of security – you have clean running water; an abundance of food, heat, light, shelter and all the comfort and luxury anyone could want. The poorest and most downtrodden in our culture live like kings compared to other parts of the world.' The two men stared at each other in silence.

'And,' Khalid continued, 'you're kept safe. No-one is going to come to your home and murder you and your family while you sleep. You have the right to a fair trial and be treated with dignity and respect – which makes you blind to the real world. It makes you soft, weak – ignorant! Which leads to selfish and sinful endeavours – crime, drugs, promiscuity and a complete breakdown of social and moral order.'

'It's called freedom! And I'd rather have this way than what you would have. I'm finished apologising to you and justifying my life. I don't believe in a god – so what? When I die, if you're right I'll burn in hell, won't I? Until then I'll live my life however I see fit, you psychotic little bastard!'

Khalid smiled again. 'Hit a nerve have I? It's funny how you reacted with anger when faced with the truth.'

'The truth?'

'Yes.'

'The truth is that you're a very disturbed young man, who's mummy and daddy didn't show him enough love, so now he wants to punish the world – a bitter, twisted excuse for a human being!'

Khalid gave a laugh of pure amusement. He genuinely thought this was funny. 'You really think that's what this is about! You've been watching too many films.'

'So it's not?'

'No. I do hate my parents, but not because they didn't love me. No. They did and still do love me. I hate the people they are. My father works for a large corporation, he's very good at his job – so much so that it became his sole focus, which meant he was away on business a lot, usually with one of many of his young assistants. This gave my mother the opportunity to indulge in her favourite pastime – British soldiers from the nearby barracks.'

'Is that why you're here, in Britain?'

'No. My parents' affairs are part of the wider problems of the West. They just went along with it because our society says it's OK to be adulterous. It has become normal, accepted behaviour.'

Andy thought of some of the people at his office. Despite Khalid's hatred, he wasn't wrong. Cheating and infidelity had become an accepted part of modern life.

'But that still doesn't mean they deserve to die.'

'In your opinion. Through my parents failings I saw what was wrong. We are expected to live our life in a certain way. We grow up, we get a job, we get married and have children, then we die.'

'That's life, though. We all die.'

'No, we live a pointless, empty life – then we die.'

'Is that how you found faith?'

'Yes. But I wouldn't expect you to understand.'

'Why not?'

'Because you have no faith – no belief in anything other than money and materialism.'

'You're wrong. I do believe in certain things. I'm not religious but I believe there are things that transcend religion and connect all the peoples of this world.'

'Like what?'

'Love,' said Andy simply. 'The love between a parent and a child, the love between a man and his wife, the love of a real friendship. I don't have to believe in any god to know these things are a very real force in this world.'

'The only love that matters is god's love!'

'I don't believe in god,' said Andy. 'I believe in freedom, the right for every person to make up their own mind and make their own choices.'

'Spoken like a true American,' Khalid sneered.

'Yes, it is. When I was at university I did a module called 'American studies', with the idea that they had, and still have, the biggest economy on earth, so one day I may have to do business with them. And for all their faults, what that country was founded on, the principles behind the War of Independence, still ring true to this day.'

'Oh really? And what's that? Greed, greed and more greed. Imperialism through finance and franchises – consumerism run wild?'

'NO! The founding fathers of the United States said, "We hold these truths to be self-evident, that all men are created equal, that they are endowed by their creator with certain inalienable rights, that among these are life, liberty and the pursuit of happiness." I agree with those words completely, and those words are still true, over two hundred years later.'

'Uttered by men who kept slaves!'

'That doesn't mean the principles were wrong.' Andy had had enough. He wasn't going to get through him. Some men you just can't reach. Some men won't listen to reason, and to some men, tolerance and understanding are alien concepts. That's why they always lose.

'I know you're not afraid to die, so there's no point threatening you with this,' he said, raising the gun slightly. 'But for once, just listen. When I was at uni I also read about a guy called Voltaire. Ever heard of him?'

'No.'

'Well, he was an 18th Century French writer and philosopher, and he said something that kind of sums up Western civilisation.

'Oh and what's that?'

'He said, "Even though I disagree with what you have to say, I'd fight to the death for your right to say it", and that, my deluded little friend, is why people like you will never ever get your way. Because there are people all around the world, of all nations, colours and faiths – even Islam – who agree with that sentiment.' Khalid didn't say a word, but just looked at Andy.

'And you know what?' Andy pursued, 'You're not even a real Muslim. You've got no understanding of Islam. You're just a fake.'

Without warning Khalid leapt at Andy, yelling, 'ALLAH AKHBAR!'

A single gunshot rang out and the sound reverberated around the small, confined space. At the exact same moment, both men felt the floor move beneath them. They were falling. The lift was falling.

19

Inside the lift gravity disappeared and reappeared. The lift was plummeting down the shaft and the men's stomachs and blood streams acted in accordance with nature.

People who have had a near death experience claim that life flashes before your eyes. They say time slows and snapshots of life play in front of your eyes. That was the sensation Andy felt as the lift plummeted to the ground. He saw the first Christmas he could remember, putting a mince pie and a glass of sherry out for Father Christmas, and a carrot for Rudolph. He remembered his father tossing pancakes on Shrove Tuesday. The recollection of his first day at school – building blocks, and the old tobacco tin that he took home with words on paper for him to learn. The family cat, run over when they moved house. He remembered the smell of his new bedroom furniture from MFI, birthday parties, family Christmases, Superman, Indiana Jones. He saw his first day at high school and fleetingly remembered how scared he was. The vividness of it all – his first crush, learning about sex, his first cigarette, stolen from his friend's mother's ashtray. The first time he was drunk – Hooch and Labatt's Ice. Buying his first album. The music of Blur and Oasis. His mum waking him up and telling him Tony Blair was Prime Minister. Princess Di's funeral. The first time he kissed a girl. Smoking a furtive cigarette out of his bedroom window. His high school phase of getting up at six o clock and going for a run, losing his virginity, sitting his GCSEs. This is it; you're going to die.

His first day at university, Tess's hair, the birth of Jake and Maggie. It's all over; you're going to die. The images tumbled through his mind: his graduation, Tess's smile, falling in love, the Rolling Stones, his wedding day, taking Jake to the pictures for the first time. This is it. The end.

Starting his job, buying the house, getting promoted. Oh God, you're going to die.

He pictured laughing with Tess and the kids – their holidays and the sun setting over the Mediterranean. I'm going to die. I'm never going to see my wife or my kids again. Emotions rushed in on him – love, hate, fear, envy, lust. I don't want to die. I'm going to miss Jake's assembly. It's all over. Is there something more? I don't want to die. I don't want to die. Oh God, I don't want to die.

He felt his stomach churn as the lift reached terminal velocity.

As if from another world, he heard the voice of Josef Reiniger – the man called Khalid was gone. 'Mother!' he called.

Andy saw the real man for the first time. Andrew Baker's eyes met his companion's, and in them he didn't see hatred, pain or violence – not even faith. The only thing he saw in the young man's eyes was his own fear reflected back at him. He held out his hand. The young man reached out and grasped it. Andrew Baker grasped back and the two men held hands, as they arrived at oblivion together.

20

Bob Fitzpatrick walked alone through the busy London streets – he had been wandering for hours. He couldn't tell if he was in shock or if it was something else. He had never seen a dead body before – not a real one anyway. Yes, he'd seen dead people at funerals, in an undertaker's chapel, and even in hospital, but he had never seen anything like the ones he had seen at work that morning. It was one thing to see someone who'd died in a bed, or been laid out by an undertaker. There was still a little dignity in that, but the same couldn't be said for the poor bastards in that lift. It wasn't natural – all twisted and broken. Not natural at all. The fear on their faces. He never knew the human body was so fragile and soft.

Why? Why did the lift drop? There were backup systems for if anything failed. Why didn't the brakes come on? Bob had always thought of himself as a simple man, with simple needs. He had never really thought about the bigger picture – at least not until this morning. He had never been spiritual – never had any faith. He'd stopped believing in God a long time ago, if he ever did at all. Most, if not all, religions taught that sodomy was a sin – *The Bible*, *The Qur'an*. They both said that just by being who he was, Bob was committing sin. For all his adult life Bob had only been in a church for weddings, christenings and funerals. He'd never even laid eyes on a copy of the Qur'an. Now though, after what had happened this morning, he had to wonder.

Was it an act of God? Or just bad luck and coincidence? He wasn't sure which prospect frightened him more. The rational side said that it was bad luck and just a tragic turn of events. The other side, however, said that maybe, just maybe, it was something else. Was there a God, any god? A supreme being with infinite power over the world? And if there was, what was it? Who was right? The Christians, the Muslims, the Jews, the Buddhists? Well, there was a Muslim in the lift, that much he knew. He doubted very much the other guy was too. Did the other guy believe in God? Was he a Christian? An atheist? Who was right? If there was a god, whose side was he she or it on?

Bob's head hurt from all the questions. He was driving himself crazy. Just shock, he thought. Just shock. The paramedics said he was OK to drive, and the police said he should go home – they'd be in touch soon. But he didn't want to. Go home and do what? Watch the morning news; feed the dogs, talk to Jimmy before he left for work, then go to bed as he usually did after a night shift? Act like it was normal day? It wasn't a normal day. Two men were dead. One of them was a terrorist who was planning on who knows what. Murder – that's what. The police said they didn't know what he was planning to do – they suspected blow himself up on a train, a bus or the tube. What if the lift hadn't dropped? What if it had gone straight down, no problem? Bob would have said good morning to both of them, he would have told them to have a good day as he did to all the other residents… But

for some reason though, through an act of God or just luck, that didn't happen. Instead the lift broke down, stopped, then dropped to the ground, killing both men. It was horrific – terrifying. Bob had never experienced anything like it – the sound as it came hurtling downwards.

Over and over he asked himself why the brakes hadn't kicked in? Bob understood enough to know that all lifts had a fail-safe.

If for some reason all the cables holding the lift snapped, then brakes fitted to the lift itself would automatically deploy, stopping the lift from falling.

The mathematical odds against this happening were astronomical. The odds alone of the cables snapping were about the same as that of being struck by lightning. And then the brakes failing – well, not the brakes, but the computer that controlled the mechanism – Jesus, this was too much to take in.

Bob came to a little park – a little oasis of green in the mass of grey. He sat down on a bench, lowered his head and ran his fingers through his hair, trying to make sense of it all. The image of the men in the lift kept creeping back in – the expressions on their faces, the fear, the terror.

He reached into his pocket to get his cigarettes and lighter – the gold one that Jimmy had bought him a few Christmases ago glinted in the morning sun. Jimmy had had his initials engraved on it... would that be all that was left? His name, carved on a piece of stone in a graveyard? Death had never frightened him before – it was something he always thought wouldn't bother him. A lot of his friends were bothered by it – the passing of time and getting older does that to some people. They come face to face with their own mortality and begin to regret some of the things they did or didn't do. Not Bob though – to him death was far in the future, at home, in bed, with Jimmy at his side – and he would just go to sleep, forever.

Bob lit his cigarette and put the packet and lighter back in his pocket. Suddenly he was scared of dying – not the pain or the physical side of death, but the unknown. What happens when you die? Something... nothing? He thought about what it would be like to die – to take his last breath. Was there something after death? If so, was it heaven and hell? Or something else? Or did you just fade away into oblivion? Like being put under anaesthetic. Was that what death was like? He remembered the few times he'd had an operation – one minute you were awake, then you were asleep and then you woke up, with no memory of what happened in between. Some people talk about near death experiences and seeing a white light. What was that? If there is a god – any god – what happens to all the souls? And what about animals? Did Bob's dogs have souls? When they died, would they go to heaven?

Or was it all bullshit – a fairytale people told themselves to stop them being afraid of death? Was all religion based on that – mankind's fear of dying? One big, fucking lie. Stop it, he thought. Where is this getting you?

Bob needed a drink. He left the park, hailed a cab and asked the driver to take him to his own local, for which he had to give a postcode, as the driver's first language certainly wasn't English. His local pub was only a few minutes walk from his home, and he could come back for his car the next day. As the cab wove it's way out of the city centre, Bob's mind went over the events of the past few hours. It all started with the bloody lift breaking down, then it crashed to the ground – and then there was the absolute chaos that followed.

After everyone realised what had happened, the inspector and the officers flew into action, and in no time the Four Freedoms Tower was awash with blue lights and uniforms – the fire brigade, the armed response unit, paramedics and the bomb disposal unit. The building's manager was called in and residents informed and evacuated. Hours had passed, but it felt like minutes. The first job was to defuse the bomb in the lift. Bob had been in a daze the whole time while the paramedics were checking him over, so he wasn't sure what time this happened. The next he knew he was finishing his statement to police in the back office.

'Well, I think that's it for now Mr Fitzpatrick. Obviously there will be a full investigation and we may need to speak to you again.'

'OK,' Bob nodded. The police left the office and the building's manager came in.

'Jesus, Bob! Are you ok?'

'I'm all right – just a little bit shook up. What time is it?'

The building manager looked at his watch. 'Half nine.

'Is it?' Bob was still dazed.

'Yeah. Look mate, as soon as the police have finished with you, get yourself home. We can handle all this. Take as much time as you like, there's no rush for you to come back in.' He placed a hand on Bob's shoulder and gave a comforting squeeze.

'Thank you.'

'Are you OK to drive?'

'I don't know, maybe I....'

'It's OK. Leave your car here. Come back for it tomorrow.'

Bob looked at the young face in front of him.

'Bob, listen, I know we don't see eye to eye on a lot of things, but I just want you to know that I really appreciate the work you do and I do value your opinion. We all do.'

'Right. Thanks. Thank you... er...'

'Get yourself off home, Bob. Do you want us to call you a cab?'

'No, no. I think I'll walk.'

'Which way now, mate?' the cab driver shouted through the glass, breaking his daydream. Bob looked round to get his bearings. They weren't that far from his house or the pub.

'Just there on this corner is fine, thank you. How much do I owe you, fella?' Bob paid the driver, got out of the cab and took a deep breath of the crisp morning air. Not that it was morning any more. He checked the time on his phone – 12:15. The pub would be open now, and it would be quiet, apart from the usual midday reprobates. There was a time when he used to hate going in straight pubs – how times change. Now it was the other way round, and he hardly went into a 'gay' bar any more. They were full of gays – well, young queens, anyway – poncing about, screaming like animals, dressed like idiots with wacky hairstyles. Bob wasn't sure why he so disliked the young gay men he came across – was it just his age? Or was he jealous of the fact that they had the things he had always wanted handed to them on a plate. They never had to hide. Never had to march for basic rights such as legality and legitimacy. When he was a young man, being gay was illegal and faggot-bashing was an approved pastime of young thugs up and down the country. And now the current generation of gay men and women were becoming exactly what those bastards thought being gay was – camp, loud, and all the other clichés. Just because he was gay, Bob didn't feel the need to wear it as a badge, to mince about and think the world owed him special recognition, just because he was gay. He never wanted a parade – he was never proud of being gay. To him that was like being proud of being a man and having a penis. To Bob the notion was ridiculous and he said as much to a young gay guy once. He immediately jumped down his throat, and started insulting him. It wasn't what the kid was saying – it was the anger and venom in his voice that shocked Bob. Just because he held a different opinion from his, the kid had spoken to him as if he was a mortal enemy – completely over the top and reactionary. But that was the way of the modern world. Today, if you held a different view or opinion from the majority, people hit the roof – about anything, politics, religion, race – Christ, even bloody football.

Bob thought of his dad, and wondered what would he make of it. He had fought in the Second World War for freedom of speech and expression – what would he make of a country where people were vilified for holding a different point of view? It was ironic, his father was one of the most homophobic men Bob had ever met, yet he risked his life for freedom – the same freedom that allowed Bob to love whom he chose and not have to be afraid. It was the same freedom that allowed that aggressive kid to dress how he wanted, dye his hair any colour he wanted. The same freedom that allowed the guy in the lift to believe what he was doing was the work of god.

Bob thought of his father and war, and what the police found in the pocket of one of the men in the lift. It was an old soldier's cap badge, dating from the War. Why did he have that? Who gave it to him? Did someone he knew fight for freedom and liberty, the same as his dad?

Then he thought of a gay kid he had met, who ranted about how the gay community should have unity, and it was because of people like Bob that there was still discrimination. Bob just walked away. The kid didn't understand.

It was the hatred, the fear and the bigotry that Bob couldn't take. Yes, he found men sexually attractive – so what? Get over it – he was still a human being. Everyone was. That was it for him – all he needed. Maybe it was a generation thing – his 'straight' friends all whinged and moaned about their kids having no respect and not having a clue. The word 'straight' really did get his back up – it was what it implied. The opposite of straight was bent, it was a derogatory term – bender, bent, bend over. The youth of today didn't seem to have a problem with that – that was acceptable. Maybe he was just a grumpy old man. Maybe it was a side effect of getting old.

He lit a cigarette and headed for the pub – the Cromwell, where he'd been drinking for years. He opened the door and went into the vault. It was nearly empty, apart from a few workmen having an early lunch in the corner and a couple of the regular dross at the bar, which included Geoff, propped up on his usual perch at the end of the bar. He was the original working-class hero – scruffy, never done a days work in his life, but had opinions on everything. A benefit cheat philosopher is what they called him. Bob just thought he was scum.

'Aaay, Bobby! How are ya, mate? Seen your place on the news. What you bin doin', hey, hey?

'What?'

The barman pointed at the TV in the corner. 'They've been on about your place all morning, Bob.' Sure enough, there was the Four Freedoms Tower on the screen.

'The lift broke down in the early hours of this morning. Police are calling it mechanical failure, pending a full investigation. They have confirmed that two men were in the lift at the time, and both were pronounced dead at the scene, however they couldn't release their identities until their families had been notified.'

Bob stared at the screen, astounded. 'Bloody hell' he muttered under his breath. He realised in all the confusion and chaos of the past few hours he hadn't even rung Jimmy to let him know he was OK. He hadn't even checked his phone to see if Jimmy'd rung. He pulled his phone from his pocket – four missed calls and a text. All were from Jimmy. He opened the text message, which read: 'Seen the news, I know you're not hurt, rang the FFs b4. I'm here if you need me. Take your time. Luv u xxx.'

Bob smiled. God, he loved that man. Jimmy knew Bob better than he knew himself.

'What ya havin', Bob?' from the landlord.

'Give us a pint of mixed and a large brandy please.' Bob took a seat at the bar and got his wallet out ready to pay.

'Here you go, Bob.'

'And your own, mate.'

The landlord gave him his change and Bob took a sip of the brandy. It was a Napoleon, but he had always preferred Jerez after he got a taste for it on his many holidays in Spain. A couple of years ago a British supermarket started doing Spanish Jerez brandy, but it was never as good as the real thing. Most pubs served French brandy, and it would have to do. It tasted good anyway, and was most welcome after the morning he'd had.

In no time the brandy was gone and he was halfway through his pint, and he went outside for a smoke. The new smoking shelter was nice – there were even roof lamps that kept you warm in winter and smart decking. The decking was a nice touch. Smoking indoors was a distant memory, but he still missed it. It was part of going to the pub – a pint and fag. Nothing like it. Those faces crept back into his head – twisted, broken. Stop it, stop it! Think about something else – anything else. He took a large gulp of his pint of mixed. That was the only thing his father left him – a taste for mixed. Not many pubs served it any more – certainly none of the new bars or clubs. It was a working-class thing – a relic from the past, with a mix of half mild and half bitter. He finished his cigarette, took a last gulp of his pint and went back inside.

'Give us another mixed please, Ian – and whatever Geoff's drinking.'

'That's too kind of you, Bob. You're a gentle-man and a scholar.' Geoff was already half cut. What a life, Bob thought – doing nothing but getting pissed everyday at the taxpayers' expense.

Bob turned round to see what was on the TV. It was still about the Four Freedoms. 'Can we change the channel please, Ian? I've seen enough of that place today.'

'Yeah sure. No worries.' The landlord changed the channel – some football analysis on a sports channel.

'So, come on, what happened, Bob?' The landlord was understandably curious.

'At work? The lift broke down and then it just…'

'Do they know why?

'No, there'll have to be a proper investigation.'

'It's fucking bad karma, that,' Geoff opined from his perch.

'You got that right – bloody bad start to the day. What do YOU reckon happened, Bob?'

'An act of God, that was,' Geoff cut in.

'What?' Bob said.

'NO, NO NO! HE SHOULDN'T BE ALLOWED TO PLAY IN THE FUCKING SUNDAY LEAGUE, LET ALONE THE PREMIERESHIP!' yelled one of the workmen, completely drowning out Geoff.

'What did you say just then, Geoff?'

'What I was saying was that…'

'YOU FUCKING PRICK!' said one of the workmen, pushing one of the others off his chair. The other one got up and threw a punch at his assailant, which missed. They began to bear hug each other and struggled round the vault, knocking over glasses, chairs and tables.

'Come on lads, don't do this. You're mates! Not over the bloody football!' said the third man with the two gladiators.

The fighters smashed into the fruit machine in the corner then headed towards the bar – fists, headlocks, kicks to the shins.

'Come on lads, STOP!' pleaded the third man.

'EVEN THE GODS OF FOOTBALL HAVE THEIR ZEALOTS,' Geoff commented gleefully, leaning over to get a better view of the action.

'RIGHT! ENOUGH! Ian said smashing a baseball bat on the bar which made them to stop just long enough for their colleague to step between them.

'OUT!' Ian said, pointing his bat at the door.

'Come on lads calm down, let's go.'

'It's all right. I'm goin'. Don't wanna be near this prick!'

'Don't wanna be near you either.'

'I'm sorry about this, mate,' said the other workmen to Ian. 'Really sorry. Here's our details. Call this number about any damage caused, it'll come out of their wages.'

'You what?' yelled one of the fighters.

In the chaos of the fight, Bob hadn't noticed that he'd spilt his brandy over himself. 'Shit.' He went to the gents to clean up, and when he got back to the vault the workmen were just leaving.

'The human race doesn't stand a chance, does it, Ian?' Geoff remarked. Ian was getting Geoff another drink.

'What can I get you, Bob? On the house. Sorry about all that nonsense.'

Bob got on his stool again.

'It's all right – not your fault. A brandy please.'

'I was just saying to Ian, Bob, look what happens when opposing forces can't live together.'

'What?'

'When two opposing forces – in this case dickheads who support different football teams – can't be in the same place. It's the place itself that suffers. Look at the mess they made. What chance do we have if we resort to violence over trivial things like football?'

'What do you mean?'

'Well, Bobby, it's quite simple. If human beings feel the need to hurt each other over a sport – an entertainment – what chance do we have when it comes to the big things?'

'What big things?' Bob pursued.

'What big things? Politics. Race. Nationality. Sexuality.' Geoff paused and raised an eyebrow at Bob.

'Then you've got the fucking H bomb – religion! Caused more shit than a farm full of pigs, he has'

'He has? You mean God?'

'Yeah God – or whatever name we choose to call him – Allah, Vishnu, Buddha, the Force!'

'You religious, Geoff?' asked Ian. He smiled at Bob – a knowing smile that was communicated without words.

'Sometimes.'

'I don't think it works like that, mate. I think you ether believe in God or you don't.' Ian insisted.

Bob just sat and sipped his brandy.

'Really? Ever been on a cancer ward? I bet every man jack in there prays at some point, whether they believe in God or not. There was an old saying in the army we used to use about God. 'There's no atheists in fox holes', and it's true, I can assure you!'

Bob looked at Geoff. 'You. – you were in the army?'

'Heh, yeah. Once upon a time. I know you wouldn't think it to look at me. But in another life I was a soldier – 2nd Battalion Parachute Regiment, six years.'

Bob glanced at Ian, and they both stared incredulously at Geoff.

'Really?' Ian queried.

'Yes really. Two tours of Belfast, then off to the Malvinas for Operation Corporate.'

'To where?' Bob asked.

'Isla Malvinas –better known as the Falklands.'

'Jesus! You were in the Falklands?'

'Yeah, and I can tell you that at Goose Green we ALL prayed – even me. And I bet the two guys in your lift prayed too, Bob. Doesn't matter how you choose to live life, when death is staring at you, you become so desperate to live that you'll cling to anything. It's the fifth freedom'

'You mean the fourth freedom?' said Ian. 'Like Bob's place.'

'He's right, Geoff. It's four freedoms. President Roosevelt in the States gave a speech once, talking about the four inherent freedoms everyone everywhere should have. They put them up in our reception and I see them every shift.

Geoff smiled. 'You know what they are, then?'

'I do,' said Bob archly.

'Go on then, enlighten us.'

'All right. The four freedoms are: freedom of speech, freedom to worship, freedom from want, and freedom from fear.'

'I never knew that,' said Ian. 'Is that why your place is called The Four Freedoms?'

'Yeah, they thought it would be poetic in this day and age.'

'Wow, I like that. It's very… I don't know… but it makes sense, though. You can't really argue with the sentiment of it.'

'I think it was more to do with who was paying for it than anything else,' Bob proffered.

'So which one did you mean, Geoff?' Ian asked, 'You mean freedom from fear – the fourth one?'

'No, the fifth freedom that FDR never mentioned. The fifth one is freedom from death.'

'Freedom from death?' Bob was mystified. 'How does that work then – we all should live forever?'

'Something like that. It all depends on your point of view and how you look at it.'

'Come on then, tell us you grand theory, professor' Ian said.

All three men smiled, and Bob took another sip of brandy.

'OK, I'll play. The fifth freedom IS freedom from death – or, more importantly, the fear of death. It's why we have religion.'

'Is it now?'

'Yeah, the human condition.'

'The what?'

'We are, everyone of us, born knowing that one day we will die.' Geoff took a large gulp of his pint. 'There's many thing that divide us, like I was saying before – class, politics, skin colour, language, gender, sexuality – but the one thing that no-one, no-one, can get away from is the fact that we all end up the same way in the end. Death is the one thing that unites us all as a species.'

'Jesus. A bit deep for this time of the day, mate' said Ian. 'So what about God? Where does he fit into it all?'

'Do you know what all religions have in common? They all say that this life isn't the end – that there is something after – heaven, hell, reincarnation, becoming one with the universe. It's a way of getting to the fifth freedom.'

'What do you think, Bob? Do you believe in God?' said Ian.

'I don't know. Maybe. It's not something I think about.'

'It's not something many of us think about until we're in the shit,' Geoff said, smiling.

'No atheists in fox holes, eh?' said Ian.

'No there's not.'

The three men sat quietly for a few seconds.

'Do YOU believe in God, Geoff?' Bob went on. 'You must have seen some horrible things. How do you cope with it?'

'With this mostly.' Geoff lifted his pint, shaking it slightly.

'But do you believe?'

'Truth is I'm agnostic. I just don't know. I've seen shit that no-one should see. But let me tell you, at the end, everyone is terrified, whether they have faith or not. I've seen it. Most of the time I think religion is all a crock of shit – all of 'em. A fairy-tale to help us cope with death, a comfort to give us hope – the hope that it all means something and isn't all pointless.'

'What?'

'Life.' Geoff took another gulp of his pint. 'But then sometimes, just sometimes, things happen that make you wonder. When every one of my kids was born I got this feeling – an indescribable feeling of joy and happiness, I suppose. Is that a divine experience? Fuck knows. But have you ever seen the sun rise over the Med? Or the way the clouds look on a summer's day? You get that same feeling of wonder – and I think all that can't be an accident.'

He finished off his pint and placed the glass on the bar with purpose.

'Right lads, I'm off. Need to go to the job centre. Got an appointment. Nice talking with you.' And Geoff headed for the door.

'See you later, Ian.' He passed Bob and patted him on the shoulder. 'Bob…

The door closed behind him and he was gone. Bob finished his brandy.

'Want another, Bob?'

'Go on then. I need one after that.'

'Yeah, he gets like that when he's had a few. No idea he was a squaddie, though.'

'I know, hard to believe. Still you never can tell – people are funny.'

'Yeah, they are.' Ian handed Bob his drink and turned the TV over to a music channel. A few people – probably office workers – came in and Ian went to serve them, leaving Bob with thoughts

He smiled to himself on the inside. Funny things, people. He didn't know if it was the alcohol or the conversation, or something else, but he felt a little better.

Ian had finished serving, and was putting glasses on the shelves.

'You goin' on holiday this year, Bob? Got anything booked?'

'No, not yet. We'll probably get a last-minute deal. better that way sometimes.' And Ian went to serve another customer. Bob sat in silence, finished his drink and made to leave.

'See ya soon, Ian.'

'You too, Bob. Take care mate.'

The bright light outside forced Bob to squint – why did that happen when you left a pub? He headed for home, and as he turned the corner he saw his house. Home again. That's where it began, last night when he left for work. Nothing had changed – it was all still the same – the front door, his flowers.

He walked through the door and went into the living room, put his keys, phone and cigarettes on the mantelpiece as he always did. He threw his coat on the couch. Looking round the room it hadn't changed at all since he left the night before. He went into the kitchen to make a brew – his cup, half full of cold tea was still on the side. He boiled the kettle and picked up his cigarettes from the front room. He was only allowed to smoke in the kitchen – it was his own little space. A brew and a fag – the little things.

He felt strange. He felt that somehow the world HAD changed. However, he looked around and everything was just how he left it. He was back at the beginning, and it felt good.

The End.

Author's Note

Firstly I hoped you enjoyed this work as much as I enjoyed writing it. The origins for Dividing Lines can be traced back to when I worked security for a large investment bank. The head of corporate security had purchased the official report into the 7th July terrorist attacks on London and it made for very interesting reading.

As a human being I find the concept of suicide bombers deeply disturbing and in fact disgusting. As a writer I find it fascinating. What is going through a persons mind when they strap a bomb to themselves and walk into a crowded place and press that button? What is the motivating factor? Faith? I really don't think it is, if it was faith in a religion or a set of ideals by itself I don't think we would have suicide bombers or even mass murderers.

And if you think hard on the issues, is there any real difference between an Islamic suicide bomber, a kamikaze pilot or a lone gunman such as Anders brevik?

And it was thinking along these lines that inspired the story of Andy Baker and Josef Reiniger.

What if you could sit down and actually talk to a person who was willing to kill themselves and hundreds, maybe even thousands of people for something they believe? What would you say? What would they say? Would it turn violent?

There are no definitive answers to these questions because we are all different which, is the main theme of this novel. We're a product of our environment and experiences, all the things that make us who we are and make us unique.

Or are we? Are we all connected on a very deep and fundamental level?

Again the answer to this question depends entirely on you, your beliefs and worldview.

I tend to veer on the side of the latter. From my own personal experiences I know only too well that human beings share the same blood regardless of race, religion, politics, class, gender or sexuality and all the other things that cause conflict on our planet.

I also know that human nature it split evenly between the capacity for good, and the other thing.

There are many theories, dogmas and doctrines pertaining to human nature and behaviour and the meaning of life, both spiritual and scientific, so which one is right?

The answer is of course down to you.

Neil Blower.

ND - #0458 - 270225 - C0 - 198/129/26 - PB - 9781908487476 - Gloss Lamination